Praise for

"Terry Lander has done it vibrant characters and a v ... .ve read and loved most of his tomes, and *Monster Jackpot* is quite possibly my favourite. Another blisteringly entertaining ride from Terry Lander. A must-read for everyone. As Lander himself wisely says, 'The house always wins, so invest in your own house.' Well, I say invest in *Monster Jackpot* first. It will brighten your whole week."
— James Mullinger, Author and Star of *Brit out of Water*

"A very tightly-told, heartbreaking story. There's a lot of desperation reflective of what so many people are going through right now, but it is matched with hope and promise."
— Michael Spicer, Star of *The Room Next Door* and *Before Next Door*

"Compelling, fast-paced, and relentless, *Monster Jackpot* is a pitch-perfect exploration of what happens when those of us who have never had money suddenly get it. At times brutal and at others intimate, it is filled with, as Freya puts it, 'constant reminders of relative poverty,' and reveals, as Bradley comes to realise, that being rich isn't necessarily freeing. This is not a story about how money corrupts, but how it divides—us from each other and from ourselves. I ended up totally immersed in this belter of a story. Superb stuff."
— Charlie Carroll, Author of *The Lip*

"*Monster Jackpot* is an entertaining cautionary tale spun around the once rare now increasingly commonplace nightmare of problem gambling and its personal consequences. Not lacking a comic touch, Terry Lander embroils his characters in addiction's inevitable stew of secrets and lies to entertainingly restate the old adage to be careful what you wish for."
— Barney Farmer, Author of *Coketown* and *Park by the River*

"An absorbing tale of greed, desperation, and what we do to get by. The lies we tell to others and ourselves, and what drives us. Terry Lander paints a familiar picture of struggling, and hoping for an easy way out."
— Mark Hendy, Author of *Panic and the Inner Monkey*

MONSTER JACKPOT

A Novella

Terry Lander

INDIE EARTH
PUBLISHING

Edited by Flor Ana Mireles and Damien Hanson

1st Edition | 01
Paperback ISBN: 979-8-9862106-6-7

First Published May 2023

For inquiries and bulk orders, please email:
indieearthpublishinghouse@gmail.com

Also available on eBook

Indie Earth Publishing Inc.
| Miami, FL |

www.indieearthbooks.com

INDIE EARTH
PUBLISHING

Monster Jackpot

£641,992.36

A Novella

Terry Lander

Other Works by Terry Lander

Adult Fiction:

Banned

Alf & Mabel

Red Light London

Children's Fiction:

Natalie's Fiendish New Headteacher

Natalie's Return to Monster Island

Natalie's Incredible Lunar Adventure

Lewis and Bruno Face the Artificial Intelligents

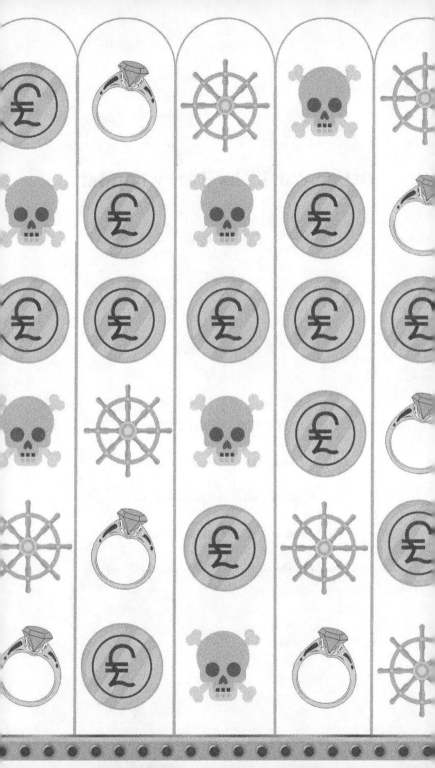

Contents

"The house always wins, so invest in your own house."

— TERRY LANDER

To my brothers and sisters,
who shaped who I am today and continue to support me.

Thank you,
Marie, Trisha, Barry, Adam, Aaron, Helen, and Linetta.

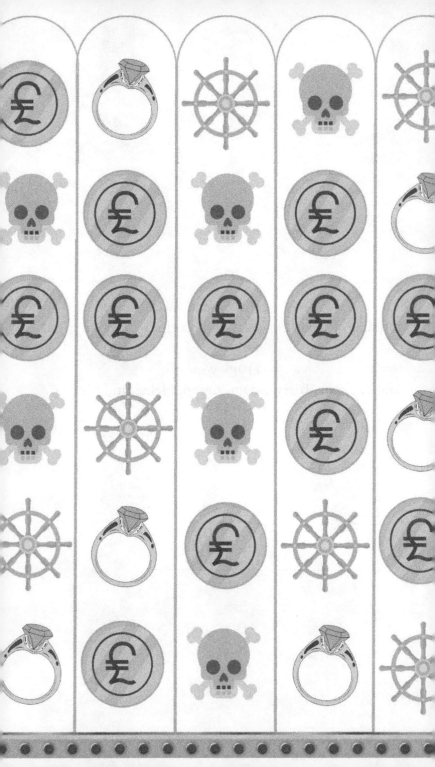

Chapter 1
BigBet

Nowhere in their vows did they promise to share a big online jackpot win, or at least that's how Bradley would spin it if his wife ever found out. He thought about how much of a cliché the situation was, spending the last fiver in his BigBet account and watching the symbols turning, listening to the clunk of each one as it stopped. He sat on the bed in their room, the early afternoon sun flowing energetically through the window, avoiding a few minor chores with a cup of tea and plate of buttered toast going cold on the table beside him as he robotically pressed the round SPIN button and started the whole process again.

Bradley had lived every day wondering if they would make the bills at the end of the month, yet three matching symbols on a game called Skeleton Crew completely changed his way of thinking. The word JACKPOT flashed in purple on the screen and he had a familiar, contradictory feeling. There was no way he was going to get the very large sum creeping up at the top of his screen, but what if he did? All he had to do was choose a symbol, one of three identical neon green skulls, and he weighed up the options in front of him. Most people were right-handed, so would they be lazy and pick the right hand icon, knowing it was the closest? Was the jackpot genuinely randomly placed beneath the symbols or was he going to lose it regardless? Without leaving too much to chance, he tapped the left-hand symbol and stared at the numbers that illuminated in front of his eyes.

£641,992.36
CONGRATULATIONS!

A vacuum cleaner started up downstairs and Bradley thought about his wife. He'd met Freya at The Cross Keys Inn, his local pub, as she'd told him that her friends had dragged her out and she was therefore standing as close to the door as it was possible to get. Bradley had spotted her wavy, blonde hair as it followed the wind every time someone went in or out of the pub. Freya had dressed in a fitted top and short skirt, both of which had been chosen by her friends to attract the most attention and it had worked, with Bradley being one of many staring at her as she drank shyly from a bottle of cider. He'd never had any trouble talking to women and gave her five minutes to settle in before he went over and introduced himself.

By the end of the night, they were sharing a tray of cheesy chips while Bradley spoke about his views on the government. She'd complimented him on how smart he appeared, his confident views on what they were doing badly seeming to make sense to her. He'd gleaned most of it from conversations at his workplace and, if analysed, would have been cobbled ideas that had been proposed to him at different points over the month before, yet he seemed to believe in himself. Freya fell in love with him almost immediately, happy to give herself over to the chatty stranger.

Freya loved to run her hands through his jet-black hair and didn't mind that he was four inches shorter than her, something her friends pointed out from the start and gently teased her for. Their marriage had been agreed and arranged within a year of meeting, Freya doing most of the legwork with the help of her mother. Her dress, cake and cars were arranged, as were the venue and catering for two hundred of their closest friends. Bradley was simply trusted with his suit hire and stag do. After the wedding, they'd enjoyed a lavish honeymoon and Bradley had bought a new car, figuring he could put it on their wedding loan and the whole lot would be paid off together. Three years later, after moving into a flat together, the balance still hadn't decreased, particularly since they'd both used credit cards to the point of needing a top up on the loan. Worse still, the new car had started to need replacement parts and was becoming a weekly nuisance.

Bradley was regularly checking the figures and then closing the banking apps when he knew how much trouble they were in. He'd added it up on a spreadsheet and the total made him numb—over twenty thousand pounds. Loan repayments were becoming a burden and every argument they had was either about money or their next door neighbour, William, and his ridiculous knowledge of housing boundary law. Discussions were more than just heated, often leading to bouts of silence which went on for days. Bradley knew it was unsustainable. He was beginning to resent his wife and believed he wouldn't have had half as much debt had they never been acquainted.

He'd had a BigBet account for as long as he remembered, years before he'd met Freya, and he'd initially used it to place tiny bets at the weekend, normally twenty team accumulators that would have paid out big if every selection had come in. He didn't really understand the odds, instead focusing on the 'win' section of his bet slip. This was more fun to him than playing the lottery as he could watch football and keep an eye on the scores, cheering every time one of his teams went in front. The sinking feeling would only come at the end of the afternoon when he counted how many teams had let him down before starting the whole process again the next week.

Bradley knew about the casino side of the site, but had put it to the back of his mind, knowing that he'd essentially be throwing money down the toilet by using it. There was no skill involved, each turn had a random outcome and any wins were generally negated by heavy losses. He was acutely aware of this. However, when he saw the size of his debt and compared it to the Skeleton Crew jackpot, he couldn't help but ignore his instinct and sank a couple of hundred pounds into the game, watching with despair every time another roll of cash disappeared from the account. He knew exactly how he was going to hide his latest gambling debts from his wife, though. He just wasn't going to tell her. Nothing was likely to change, at least until that moment the massive jackpot was confirmed.

Chapter 2

Freya

The word shy meant a lot of things to different people, though Freya never thought it applied to her. She was cautious and always thought before she spoke yet had been referred to as shy for as long as she could remember. Freya loved company and conversation, often trying to spend time with those who taught her things, or at least valued her opinion. She admitted to introverted tendencies, perhaps, but would never have called herself shy.

Boyfriends seemed easy to find for Freya and she was never short of offers. Lads in school had initially acted differently towards her, making her believe that they were a good match before showing themselves for the idiots they truly were. This made her guarded and it regularly took her a long time to open up, meaning people noticeably avoided her company and called her stuck up. This made her even more introverted, as it would anyone, at least in her opinion.

When Bradley first approached her at the Cross Keys, she was wary of the charm that seemed to come so easily to him, despite there being something different about him. He said everything she wanted to hear and seemed to be able to back up his claims, such as coming fifth in a local half marathon when he was twenty, surely too obscure a claim to invent. Freya loved the combination of apparent athleticism and genuine warmth, which led to them becoming a couple so quickly despite her previous experiences.

There was something about being in a relationship that

had changed them both, although for Bradley the changes seemed larger. Within a year, he was so far from running distances that his impressive stat was almost null and void, certainly to the point that he never spoke of it again. Freya was fine with his lack of physical fitness, but less so with his ambition to do as little as possible, putting it down to relationship comfort at first.

When it continued, Freya confided in her mother that she thought she'd broken him completely. Their own relationship was often considered strange by outsiders as Freya's mother had always acted as more of a friend to her, rarely offering advice unless it was asked for. They shopped, went to the cinema and smoked weed together, the latter drying up after Freya and Bradley got together as he hated the thought of drugs skewing their connection. Nevertheless, Freya's mother was always in the picture and often took the strain if arguments broke out between them both.

At one point, their house had become heated over the storage of condiments. Freya had always kept ketchup in the fridge, as had her mother and her grandmother, not so much a tradition but a general handing down of information through the years. Bradley had never had ketchup as a child, although his friends had kept theirs in the cupboard and he was certain that it was the correct storage technique. They were both red in the face and shouting when Freya's mother arrived, calming the situation and assuring them that it didn't really matter.

"If this is the only thing you can find to argue about, you're going to be absolutely fine," she'd concluded.

On the day that Bradley was winning on BigBet, Freya was looking around at their house in despair. He'd spent the previous night with a school friend she'd never seen before who had returned to the town for a day, and the two of them had decided to make a throne out of beer cans, eventually drinking most of a crate between them. Bradley had shooed his friend away at the end of the night, promising to clean up in the morning but being far too hungover to do so. Freya didn't have the energy to complain. Instead, she began picking up the cans before tidying away the empty packets of crisps and pizza boxes.

While Bradley and his friend caught up, her evening had been spent in bed, trying to keep out of the way by watching a box set. Her back was aching, she was yawning after being constantly woken by their laughter, and she had no expectation towards waking up to such a drastically messy house. By the time she got to the vacuum she was crying, hoping Bradley would make it up to her somehow. Instead, as she reached for the power button and unplugged her least favourite appliance, Bradley was winking at her and putting his coat on, telling her he'd only be a minute. Freya couldn't believe what she was seeing and sighed, the gesture too late for him to catch as he skipped out of the door.

After a few minutes, the doorbell rang. Freya thought that Bradley had forgotten his keys, but she opened the door to find the postman delivering yet another parcel for her husband.

She ranted to him about Bradley's extravagant spending, to which he simply replied, "Don't blame me, Love, I only bring the bloody things."

Annoyed that he couldn't even pretend to take her side, she offered insincere thanks and slammed the door, leaving him looking at the frosted glass and wondering what her issue really was.

Freya threw Bradley's latest purchase on his chair and looked around the living room and hallway, pleased with what she'd managed to achieve for the day. She was more tired than she ever believed it was possible to be, but at least her house was back to normal. The doorbell rang again, and Freya considered answering it, taking to the stairs instead, climbing towards a well-deserved break. She lay on the bed, intending to check her phone yet found her eyes closing as soon as she lay down. The room still smelled of

Bradley's late night on the booze, something she had to block out as she fell into deep sleep.

Chapter 3
Hiding The Loot

Bradley had looked up from the screen of his phone as he heard the vacuum noise moving ever closer. He had no idea how to collect the money he'd apparently won on his phone and even considered that there may have been another step, making him cautious. He closed the door to their bedroom and investigated further, taking his time to press through slowly and read every piece of information that flashed up on the screen. Sure enough, he received confirmation of his winnings and an email with further instructions. He grew concerned that Freya would discover his good fortune and make big plans, so he decided to make his way to the Cross Keys to use their wi-fi and find out how long it would be before his bank account was finally filled.

As he approached the bottom of the stairs, his mood had started to lift despite the situation not really having sunk in. He looked at Freya as he put on his coat, caught her eye and winked in a way he never had before, hoping he hadn't creeped her out. He left quickly, walking straight towards the pub without telling her where he'd gone yet knowing he was going to be longer than a minute. The weather reflected his mood, bright and sunny, unlike the young mother who was shouting at her child for dragging his feet as they walked. He chuckled quietly to himself, trying to get his head around how he would spend his winnings.

Entering the Cross Keys, Bradley made his way to the bar in the far corner of the room and ordered his usual pint of lager. His wallet was a mess of old receipts and loyalty cards, enough for him to have to rummage through to find a credit card he could use at the bar. His mind had started to spin from the size of his win and he stuttered as he thanked the bartender, keen to sit on his own and sign in to his BigBet account. Picking up his drink, he caught the eye of Tony, a lad he'd been to school with, who was regularly out without Bradley, yet sometimes joined him for a few pints—generally up until Tony was arrested for fighting. Bradley sighed and nodded, hoping he'd have no interest and carry on drinking with the group around him.

"Whatcha up to?" Tony shouted across the bar, the rest of the room going quiet as they gave Bradley a chance to answer.

Bradley muttered, "Nothing much, mate," and wandered over to an unoccupied table, turning his back on the crowd to no avail.

"It's your round, mate," Tony said with a chuckle.

Bradley rolled his eyes, knowing he'd struggle to get on his phone without a quick chat. He conceded and stood with the group for a short while, listening to the usual gossip about patrons who weren't there being under the thumb and tales of who was sleeping with who. Finally, he had a go at trying to excuse himself.

"I've got to text the missus. I've had some good news," he said cautiously.

Tony looked at him seriously. "You've won some cash; I can see it in your face."

He was known to be a bit of a poker player, yet Bradley finally found out just how good he was, at least in the lower leagues. Bradley tried to hide it, shrugging it off before finally admitting he could afford more than just a round of drinks for them all.

Tony turned to the bartender. "The rest of the night's on this guy!"

Soon, a quick trip turned into a session and Bradley knew he'd have to ring Freya. He was still anxious to check his account, yet had to hide it from the mob around him who were getting steadily more inebriated. He put his head down, drank, and kept his answers vague. In truth, most thought he'd won a couple of hundred pounds and were starting to feel guilty for cashing in on his good fortune. This meant the crowd died down and Bradley eventually found a window of opportunity to escape.

"Catch you all later," he shouted back to the remaining group members, giving the barman his credit card to settle the bill.

He'd lost over four hundred pounds already, a drop in the ocean realistically, yet more than he was planning to spend on people he thought of as less than friends.

To save face, Bradley went to the shed just outside his house, sat on a rusty barbecue and picked up a weak wi-fi signal where he was finally able to get more details. The win was confirmed in his account and the money was due to be paid into his bank within five working days. In that time, literature would arrive that would help him to decide how best to spend his money, although he would not be directly told what to do with it. Tears streamed from Bradley's face as he realised that he could pay his long outstanding bills and be debt free for the first time since he was eighteen, almost a decade previously.

Two nights with copious amounts of alcohol had started to make Bradley's head throb and he lay on the floor of the shed to calm down a bit. He thought of all the ways he could potentially tell Freya if he didn't want to hide it forever—carrier pigeon, balloon in a restaurant, over a river on a private flight—realising instead that it would probably just come out naturally one day. He visualised this as his eyes grew heavy, closing on his behalf as he rested through the tiredness. He didn't have the energy to send a message to Freya about when he was due to return, figuring that she'd understand if she really loved him. This turned out to be his last thought as he lost consciousness.

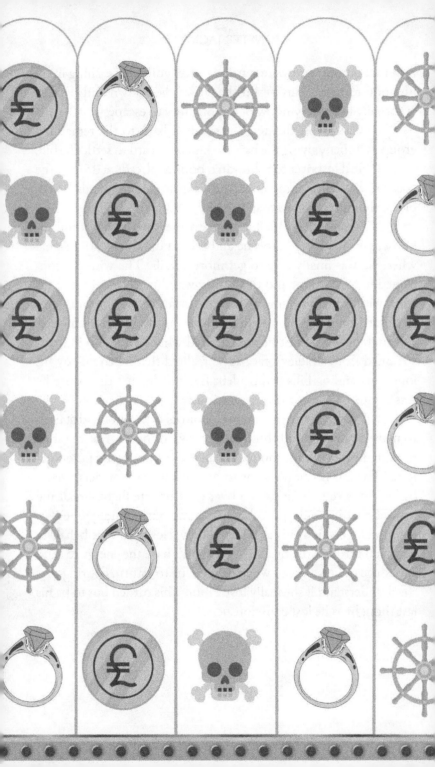

Chapter 4

Bradley's Return

A low rumble came from the bedside table, which woke Freya with a start. She darted for her vibrating phone, hoping it would be Bradley telling her at least where he'd gone. After reading a text about cheap home insurance, she sent a quick, concerned message to Bradley and wiped her eyes to wake herself up. Freya spent the next five minutes watching her blank screen, annoyed that he didn't seem bothered enough to reply.

It was early afternoon and Freya was sure that Bradley was fine, just wanting a bit of confirmation in case he'd got himself into trouble. More than once he'd come back from the Cross Keys having watched football and gotten involved in a fight—normally breaking up other drunk fans, but he'd also started a fight with Freya's ex-boyfriend despite being unprovoked. She knew she couldn't waste a day of her weekend worrying, though, as she'd be back on the spanners that Monday fixing cars for her apprenticeship while he'd have enjoyed the weekend of his life. Instead, she put him out of her mind, hoping he'd be back with at least a bunch of flowers and an apology for being out too long so they could enjoy an evening together.

Keeping them both afloat had been difficult for Freya as her apprenticeship brought in a ridiculously low wage, which was topped up only slightly with benefits. Bradley brought in around the same amount with his unemployment subsidy, keeping his payments going by applying for the minimum number of jobs and particularly targeting those he was least likely to get. They both paid half of the bills each, though Freya's account always seemed empty, particularly while she was paying off their joint loan. She knew that finishing the training would help incredibly, but also realised that it was two years away.

Freya sometimes thought about life without Bradley, whether she'd be able to cope on her own given how much time he spent pursuing his own interests. He'd never done much around the house other than trash it and he could have taken his bills with him if they split. Did she still love him after their wedding? Freya considered that her worry for his whereabouts at that moment must have been a good sign. However, her plan was to give him both barrels when he got in.

Freya was still woozy as she descended the stairs and made herself comfortable on the living room sofa, which stood between the front door and the entrance to the kitchen. The TV beeped as it came to life and she got comfortable in front of it, almost refreshed from her nap and keen to indulge in someone else's life. She loved to watch documentaries about accidents, hoping it would help her general engineering skills and therefore improve her value at work. She had a lot to catch up on having cleaned the entire house for the morning and was quietly pleased not to have Bradley there to interrupt her. Freya managed over four hours of programs and was settling into the early evening when the door finally opened, Bradley looking like he'd been in another fight when he'd simply been rolling through discomfort on the floor of their shed.

"Where the bloody hell have you been?"

Freya just caught his eye as he walked through the door and spoke before he had a chance to close it. Bradley was nursing his head and had clearly had another session which could well have been at a friend's house if not at the pub.

"I was planning to tell you, but I won't bother if you're in this mood."

His face snapped to a cruel expression and Freya huffed loudly to counter. She gave him detail on how much work she'd done, all of which was due to his unwilling attitude.

Bradley skulked upstairs, shaking his head and muttering to himself, "Looks like you've been sat on your arse all day."

The top stair creaked as Freya looked up in disbelief.

"Where do you think your shite from last night went?" she shouted, knowing there was no chance of a response.

She shook her head and went back to the TV, feeling a pang of guilt for a moment but then realising that Bradley had put that on her.

The creaking ceiling above Freya suggested that Bradley was getting into bed despite the fact they normally stayed up a little on Saturday nights, even if he had been drinking heavily. He often fell asleep, dribbling on her shoulder, while she caught up with the shows she'd missed during the week. He clearly didn't want to take part this time and so she went on normally, once more imagining how life would be different without him. A drier shoulder, for a start.

Ant and Dec appeared on the screen in front of her and were inviting their audience to text in to win a large sum of money. The amount was blurry in front of her as she concentrated on the Geordie lads, wondering if life was any better having to clean up after them. Her mind then wandered to the cash, particularly what she would do with a million pounds. A list formed in her head—buy herself a house, pay off her mum's mortgage, perhaps a new car? She loved her little Fiat 500, but had to work on it regularly. Would she get someone else to do her car? Did she trust anyone enough? Probably not. Perhaps she could supervise them.

A vibration brought her back to the present and she realised that her phone was lighting up with a text message on the coffee table. Her friend, Sue, had just come back from a holiday in Malta. Her husband had sprung it on her as a surprise. Better than a surprise beer can chair, she thought.

A holiday went straight on to her mental list, somewhere hot with decent cars to look at. Malta had some good, old, British classics such as Minis and Escorts and she'd often thought about rescuing a couple of them, driving them back and doing them up. Again, money had come into play. Would that be the first thing she did? Freya sent a quick text back to Sue and returned to Ant and Dec, who by now had finished trying to get her to call a premium rate phone number. How much of that did *they* get? She didn't really care since there was no way she could be a TV presenter.

Her eyes grew heavy during this last thought and Freya let them drop, thinking about Bradley and his day. He hadn't even let her know where he'd been, nor had he asked her about her day. This mattered less and less as her eyes closed for the last time, accents from the TV filling her ears and drowning out her thoughts at last.

Chapter 5
The Half Millionaire

The warm air of the room felt heavy on Bradley's head as he opened his eyes, looking at the clock to realise that he'd wasted most of his Sunday. He heard the TV downstairs, figuring Freya must have been to bed and gotten up early that morning. The smell of bacon lingered, though he knew not to push his luck after two consecutive sessions without a proper conversation with his wife. He couldn't remember if they'd had an argument the night before, deciding to gauge the answer from her reaction to him when he made it downstairs.

He picked out his best T-shirt from the drawer, deciding that a guy with half a million due into his account very soon probably should have something better to wear. He therefore decided to load up his credit card and pay it off once the money hit. The bar bill was already on there, so he figured a few extra pounds wouldn't cause much of an issue.

Every pint Bradley had indulged in seemed to gang up on him, the room spinning slightly as he stood up after getting dressed. He was rarely sick after drinking, yet the double session combined with whatever Tony had forced him to drink meant that he was soon hanging over the edge of the toilet, trying to get every drop into the bowl. There was a little cleaning to do afterwards, though he felt much better having unloaded a good portion of what was in his system. Freya had never made him bacon before and so he decided to treat himself to an all-day breakfast at a café, omitting the fact during their initial conversation.

"How are you, Love?" Bradley coyly shouted down the

stairs, expecting an immediate explosion from his wife.

Instead, she looked up towards him and simply uttered, "Fine," a word that was clearly loaded with emotion.

He slowly crept down the stairs as though he was avoiding waking their neighbours, looking towards Freya's stony face and smiling slightly to show that he knew he was in the wrong.

"Sorry for the drinking... I think I went a bit overboard there."

"...and?" Freya's stern expression remained after she spoke, leading Bradley to realise that he was in *deep* trouble.

"Did we argue last night? I'm so sorry, it's just that Tony..."

The mention of someone else's name was all it took to invoke the reaction he was expecting. Freya unleashed Hell, telling him that it wasn't just the drinking and lack of cleaning, but the fact they'd barely spoken all weekend. Bradley stood and watched as Freya unloaded, looking like a naughty school child as he started to realise where he'd gone wrong. She never would have gone to the pub with him, yet the fact he hadn't said he was going there seemed to be most of the problem. He thought about his BigBet account again, trying to get the information he needed, and knew he couldn't be honest about it without giving away his big win.

"I just forgot. I'm really sorry. Let me make it up to you. I need to grab a few bits in town."

"I'll get you something nice," he added while walking out the door.

Freya's face dropped as he spoke, and she realised that he was about to spend the last part of their weekend on his own. He promised to be back within a couple of hours and to devote the evening entirely to her, which seemed to calm her a little. He made sure not to wink this time as he made his way to the door, blowing her a kiss to avoid sharing his rancid breath before closing the gap behind him.

Breakfast and T-shirts were the easy part. He threw down an entire plate of bacon, sausage, and egg with all the trimmings and went for another cup of tea, something he considered a rip off normally. He'd barely noticed the change in his attitude, the hot beverage feeling free to him as it was being subsidised by his new favourite online casino. It was the first time he'd ever left a tip as he rounded up his card payment, the air around him filled with cartoon happiness as he almost danced out of the door whistling a cheerful tune.

More changes were afoot as he shunned his normal retailer, opting instead for a surf wear shop to buy his T-shirts in as he'd often pined over the California slogans and pictures of camper vans that others had worn. He didn't stop to look at the prices, bundling them all together after trying them on quickly and dropping them on to the counter for the assistant to scan. When the figure flashed up on the till, he didn't comprehend that it was equivalent to three weeks of benefits for him. Besides which, he knew he'd have to give a reduced figure to Freya anyway when talking about the price of the shirts.

Bradley contemplated a quick pint in the Cross Keys, the breakfast having sorted his head nicely. As he made his way there, he passed a jeweller that had been in town longer than he'd been alive yet he'd never once stopped to look in the window. On this occasion, a number of rings caught his eye and he decided that these were the kind of gifts that accompanied a good apology. Her engagement ring had featured diamonds and it had taken him six months to raise enough for the tiniest rock. At that point, he knew he could walk in and purchase almost anything on the shelves, studying those in the window for over five minutes as people passed by behind him.

Impressing her was his ultimate goal, picking a solitaire that was more than ten times the size of her original ring and making his way inside to hand over his card once more. He'd spent over a thousand pounds before noticing a Rolex Submariner that was strikingly similar to a fake his father had picked up on holiday in Tenerife when he was younger. He barely noticed that he'd spent eleven times the amount on the watch than the ring, again deciding to hide the actual price from his wife if she even noticed at all.

The cashier made a comment about how much Bradley was spending and suggested he sign up for store credit, although Bradley was certain that keeping it all on one card would make it easier to pay off. He thanked the cashier and lied about considering it before he left, the spring in his step in no danger of disappearing as he made his way to the pub for a swift drink.

Chapter 6

An Apprentice's Life

A knock on the door had woken Freya early on the Sunday and she'd meant to tell Bradley, forgetting when she realised that he was on his way out later that afternoon. As she opened the door, a giant man with a bald head and thick coat showed her some ID that confirmed he was from a debt collection agency. He explained that their energy bill was long overdue, a fact she'd never have known as it was part of Bradley's monthly bills. He'd never discussed it or asked to borrow money to pay it off, instead he seemingly hid the bills and left her to find out in this way.

The guy at the door was particularly brash and clearly wouldn't take no for an answer. The amount he wanted, over six hundred pounds, was well out of her budget yet she realised that something needed sorting. Freya invited him in, her offer declined as he held his position at their front door. In truth she was trying to keep him out of sight of their neighbours, though she noticed curtains twitching in the house opposite them. Freya was close to tears as she tried to figure out where she could get the money from, turning over every drawer in the house to find whatever funds may have been squirrelled away. Failing catastrophically, all she could offer was a payment plan.

"Sounds agreeable. You seem like an honest girl," he said finally.

Freya stirred in frustration on the inside as she figured he could have offered that as a starting point to save her time. All she could realistically afford was a tenner a week and he continued to study her carefully for sincerity before asking for a signature to set up the plan. Finally, he suggested increasing the payments as quickly as possible before concluding their meeting. Freya closed the door behind him and went back around the house to replace the drawers one by one before collapsing on the sofa and sobbing.

Bradley clearly hadn't heard the commotion as it was hours later when he got up and left the house. Watching him leave, Freya's heart sank to think that she'd be on her own once more. She remembered the caller half an hour later and decided to message Bradley, the quick reply from him claiming that he'd simply forgotten about it and would sort it as soon as the energy company opened that Monday. His apology was accepted by Freya as the fear of the debt was lifted, although she was still annoyed at his overall performance across the weekend.

The adrenaline of a bad day had made Freya really hungry, and she was sure Bradley wasn't bringing any food home. She'd had a bacon sandwich before Bradley had left, but she couldn't wait until he got home before deciding to make herself something more substantial. Opening the cupboards, nothing seemed out of place which suggested that Bradley hadn't eaten anything while he'd been home and had probably eaten every time he'd gone out. Perusing the tins, Freya could only see two of beans, one of chopped tomatoes and another of meatballs in gravy. The single tin of tuna she'd managed to pick up while shopping had long since been used and Freya's lack of choice was starting to lower her mood even more. She coupled the tomatoes with a bowl full of pasta and grated the last square of cheese from the fridge over the hot mixture before placing it back on an empty shelf that sat above two very barren others.

Finishing her paltry meal, Freya tried to block out her hunger. The TV was showing repeats from the week just gone and she was blindly re-watching episodes of soaps that had barely kept her entertained the first time round. Her phone lit up with a message from her old school friend Darlene and it was a welcome interruption. Freya asked Darlene about every aspect of her week after filling her in on the monster who had come to reclaim their energy payments. She exaggerated slightly yet remained honest about the fear she had felt when she looked up and met his gaze. Darlene replied that he sounded fit, Freya assuring her that he was not a man who seemed to enjoy life.

After replying, Freya thought about inviting Darlene around. They'd remained good friends since their first meeting, though Darlene had often brought more drama to their conversations than Freya, who generally preferred a quieter life. When they went out together on a weekend, it was Darlene who lured Freya towards trouble, even suggesting that cheating on Bradley as a one-off was not really cheating at all. Freya often heard of people getting too drunk to remember what they were doing, and this made her wary of how much she took on board, although there were occasions where this drinking rule was broken. Freya found herself relieved to be back beside Bradley, Darlene having dropped her off on each occasion.

The thought of inviting her friend round came with a high probability that they'd end up going out together, something Freya couldn't have done if she wanted to make it to work the next day. She pushed the idea to the back of her mind and finished up her conversation, suggesting they might go out the following weekend.

Hunger pangs brought her back to reality and she went back to watching the soaps, hoping for another message from a different friend so she could potentially tell her heart-breaking story once more. Her eyes felt heavy and she decided it was best to succumb to sleep to prepare her for a showdown with Bradley, knowing she'd need to be on her toes.

The front door banged open as Bradley made his way through an hour later, the smell of food wafting through the air. Freya woke with a start, catching the smell yet containing any excitement as he often ate while he was out and went back empty-handed, the smells enough to tease his wife. Freya looked up and rubbed her eyes, seeing his silhouette in the doorway.

"Ey oop," he said cheerfully.

Chapter 7
Cubics Are For Whenever

The bags of food were starting to weigh down Bradley's arms and he bumbled through the living room to settle them on the counter in the kitchen. He'd gone from the jeweller to the Burger Up fast food restaurant on his way home, not knowing what he really wanted and ordering six different meals to share with Freya. Whatever was left could go in the fridge for their supper, he considered.

Bradley's rustling from the kitchen, joined with the smell taking over the house, enticed Freya to get up from the sofa and meet him, almost bursting into tears when she noticed how much he had in the bags. Bradley had a massive grin on his face, and he looked at his wife, feeling like Jesus on the way to feed his followers.

"Don't worry, it's not just for me. Get your mouth around something tasty!" he said before breaking into a whistle, placing a chicken burger front and centre in the fridge for later. "Don't touch that, though, or I'll have to open you up to get it back."

After placing the chicken burger, Bradley could hear weeping from the other side of the kitchen and saw that Freya was genuinely distraught.

"It was only a joke. What's up?"

Freya rubbed her eyes and stood up straight.

"You know what's up. I sent you a message. Where the hell did this lot come from? I've just tried to make a bowl of pasta with the scraps we have."

Looking confused, Bradley checked his phone and saw

that he'd missed a message from her. He apologised, grabbing a punnet of chips and loading his mouth to show how hungry he was in solidarity. He also grabbed a double bacon cheeseburger, ensuring it would be his.

Folding her arms, Freya went into detail about the debt collector and the energy bill. She told him that there was a payment plan in place, but that he'd need to pay her first before the money left her account. He nodded before she asked why he hadn't paid it in the first place.

He told her that he'd missed the first few letters, mistaking them for bank statements that he'd immediately thrown in the bin. In truth, he'd known about the debt collection agency, but hadn't realised that they would be sending someone round, not that it mattered at that point.

"It'll be sorted first thing tomorrow," he said, again omitting how he was suddenly able to pay the bill. He loaded more chips into his mouth, mumbled the word, "Tea?" and put the kettle on to boil.

"I wanted to turn this down and make you feel guilty for making me go with sod all for tea, but I can't. It smells too good. Of course you can make me tea. It'll almost make up for me facing a gorilla on your behalf today."

"Better than that..."

Bradley went into his pocket and felt around, almost pulling out the container for his watch instead of the smaller ring box. He pulled off the switch unnoticed, smiling as ever when the fuzzy green one emerged from his pocket.

"This is for you."

The rustling had stopped, and the room was silent as Freya put her hands to her cheeks.

"I don't believe it! This is mine?"

Bradley nodded, opening the box to show off the large single diamond sparkling beneath the lights. Freya put one hand over her mouth, removing it as she leaned forward to gently grasp the box.

"We can't afford to heat this place; how did you afford this?"

"I'll let you in on a little secret. It's a cubic zirconia. Much cheaper than it looks. Don't tell anyone though," Bradley said, hoping Freya hadn't noticed he was lying on the spot as he'd rarely had to do it previously.

He wasn't very good at lying and didn't enjoy it, so he cursed himself for buying such an extravagant gift following what had been a fairly tepid argument. He figured the best course of action would be to keep gifts for Freya to a minimum and enjoy the money himself, leaving a little for bills, such as the energy debt, which were bound to crop up.

The ring sparkled like Freya had never seen before, although she put it down to the cut of the stone.

"It's beautiful," she said, her voice breaking to match her tears.

At that point, she caught sight of his new watch.

"You got yourself something, too, I see."

Further lies filled Bradley's head as he struggled to pluck the right one out.

"It's a copy, don't worry. I bought it for both of us, really. I've spent so much of this weekend unaware of the time that I thought I'd get something big to remind me when I need to get back to you."

He wondered if his lies were more extravagant than the watch itself, noticing Freya's suspicious look.

"I don't believe that for a second," she said, returning to her ring in a gesture of positivity.

Freya thanked Bradley once more, loving the shine of the band as much as the sparkle of the rock. She kissed him, reminding him that he wasn't yet forgiven.

The two of them made their way into the living room where they sat and watched TV, eating most of the food that

Bradley had returned with. He couldn't believe that the two of them had eaten so much, realising how hungry his wife must have been. They often spent Sundays lazing on the sofa and mourning the return of Monday, which Freya did by talking through the cars she already had lined up to repair. Bradley thought about another day applying for jobs then wondered why he wasn't making the most of his new-found wealth.

"I think I'm going to tell the Job Centre I'm sick tomorrow," he muttered before realising that he was saying it out loud.

An argument was brewing, yet Freya was too full to move or shout. She slowly blinked, never taking her eyes off the TV, and asked him how he thought they could afford for him to carry on without a job. He told her that one day off wouldn't hurt before wondering how he'd cover himself for the rest of the week. He did some quick maths in his head and soon realised that he could actually cover a potential wage for the next 30 years, give or take a ring and a watch here and there. He also had a bar bill, t-shirts and the burgers to cover, though that left more than enough for him to enjoy his Monday. Freya said nothing as he confirmed his decision, beaming from ear to ear at the thought of a late start in the morning. He would have grabbed a beer had he been able to get off the sofa.

Chapter 8
The Ring In The Salesroom

Work bay three at Wilson's Garage was often already lit when Freya got to work, although on this Monday she arrived slightly early to show off her ring. The other five work bays were just as dark since none of the other mechanics had arrived, as expected, yet the sales team were busy preparing on the shop floor upstairs and Freya made her way towards Sheila, one of her best friends within the company. Before long, a small crowd had formed around Freya and they were all complimenting her, while Sheila looked suspiciously at the ring.

"Did you say it's a cubic?" she asked, her face showing puzzlement.

Freya looked towards her and smiled. "Aye, it's all we could afford between us, but it's beautiful."

"I agree, but it looks like a diamond to me. Were you there when he got it?"

Without missing a beat, Freya told Sheila all about the shopping trip, adding herself in to save too many questions. She couldn't answer why Bradley had come back with jewellery and so much food, so she left out as many details as possible to keep their attention on the ring. She was certain it wasn't stolen as Bradley had never been inclined to do so before, hoping he'd managed to pick it up in a sale or had cleaned up a second-hand ring. There was no way he could afford a diamond, so Sheila's suspicions were discarded as quickly as possible.

One of the head sales team members was Sawyer, who wore more grease in his dark hair than Freya had covering her at the end of a shift. He saw the crowd and made himself a coffee, pretending to ignore the hubbub. When he saw the crowd had dispersed he quickly walked towards Freya, waiting until they were out of general earshot before talking to her.

"Your man's finally stumped up for a decent rock, then?"

Due to working on cars all day, Freya never wore a ring and Sawyer had picked up on this in the past. Now that she had one to show off, he seemed even more eager to dismiss Bradley as a waster. Freya knew that, even if she hadn't been with Bradley, there was still no chance of her ending up with Sawyer. He had a reputation when she joined the company for sleeping with customers in the cars during test drives and he never seemed to quash the rumours.

"He stumped up for one years ago. This is just a sign that he still loves me. You could do with some love in your life," she said, without taking her eye off the jewellery.

"I get plenty of love, don't worry about that."

Sawyer pushed back his slimy mane and put his other hand over his crotch, thrusting to emphasise his point.

Freya laughed with pity, wondering how customers ever fell for his charms. She shook her head and made her way to the coffee machine before the first potentials walked through the door.

"You should get yourself a job in sales, keep those soft hands clean and make yourself enough for a proper diamond. That looks like cut glass to me."

"It's a cubic," she replied, to which Sawyer scoffed.

Freya finally looked up at him and narrowed her eyes, confidence building in her as she spoke.

"Besides, money doesn't interest me. Have you ever tuned a Hayabusa until it screamed beneath you, catapulting your entire body around a track, and watching the faces on people like you as you pass them without breaking a sweat?"

"I can just pay grease monkeys like you to do it for me," he arrogantly sniped, lifting his nose as he did so.

Freya chuckled and shook her head.

"That's why we'd never work, Sawyer. You have no soul."

She made her way back down the stairs to the workshop, thinking about the vehicles that were already lined up for her to work on.

As she drove the first one in, a Focus with worn front brakes, her thoughts drifted to money and how struggling day-to-day really affected her. Splitting the bills had worked out fine, yet there was very little else left for things she wanted. Freya had once bought a George's Marvellous Medicine money tin, the only symbol of the Roald Dahl books she'd adored as a child in the house, and had put a pound in it to start a savings account for a trip to Iceland. By the time Bradley made it home that day, she'd already had to use a tin opener on the can to retrieve the pound as they'd needed milk and he'd claimed that he didn't have enough to buy any. Freya kept the tin for a short while, never managing to put any more into it before she got rid of the constant reminder of her relative poverty.

Her next thought was of Sawyer. Freya had never seen him drive anything that was more than a year old and figured he got a discount through the company in the same way she could fix her own car without being charged for labour. It never seemed completely fair to her, although she'd never asked about a discount on a new car knowing that she'd never be able to afford one either way. The manner in which Sawyer strutted around the salesroom made her cringe and she thought for a second about what it may have been like to live with him, doing his washing and making sure his house was kept immaculate. She shuddered at the thought of him touching her, knowing for sure that Bradley had no worries about her deceit. Whether she was completely happy or not was irrelevant when it came to Sawyer since she could never be unhappy enough to lower herself for him.

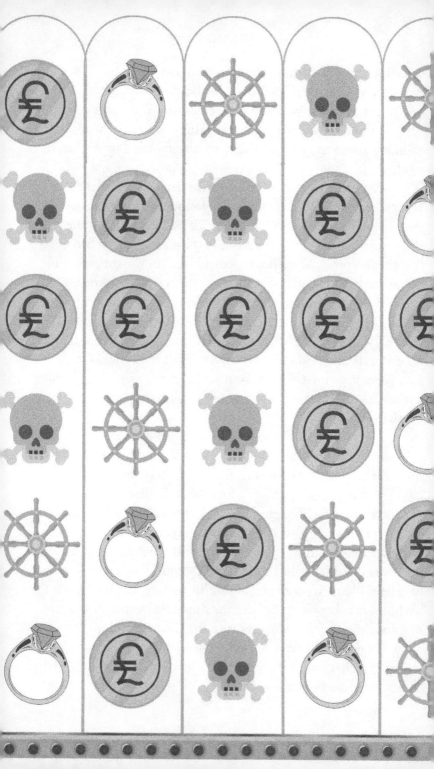

Chapter 9

Bradley's New Ride

As Freya was getting dressed to go to work, Bradley was coughing all over his phone.

"I could come in, but I don't want to give this awful cold to all the other jobseekers," he managed to splutter between bouts.

His account manager told him to rest up and put the phone down, Bradley laughing at his own performance afterwards. He then climbed back into bed, pulled the duvet right up to his chin and smirked as he closed his eyes.

Freya rolled hers at the terrible performance.

Shortly afterwards, the door closed with a bang and Freya shouted, "Bye," in a curt manner as she left the house.

Bradley started to dream about what he could do with his day, drifting off as thoughts of jet skis played in his mind. Two hours later, his phone rang with an unfamiliar number on the screen.

"Hello?"

A short silence followed before a member of the fraud team at his credit card company started to speak. They were concerned about a number of large transactions on his card, a facility he hadn't used for over twelve months previously.

"Could you confirm the transactions for me please, sir?"

Bradley listened to the list of items that had already been added to the account, confirming them all. He'd barely broken into his monster jackpot win and was looking forward to adding to the amount, something he told the caller with enthusiasm.

The enquiry was satisfied between them both, although

the call was not yet complete.

"If necessary, we could add to the credit limit on your card to allow you to enjoy your winnings before paying the balance off in full. If this is done by the end of the month, then you'll incur no interest or charges."

This thought perked Bradley up. His initial plan was to use store credit where necessary as he'd been offered by the jeweller, but this way he could keep spending and still have everything in one place. All they needed was proof of his win in the form of an email from Bigbet and, within the hour, he had a seemingly bottomless card at his disposal.

"To the lake," he said as he confirmed his approval, a plan forming in his mind.

Bradley imagined pitching up at the lake on his own, darting around for an hour and then not being able to tell anyone what he'd done. He had no real friends, only people he did favours for or those he drank with, most of whom he didn't have numbers for as they were guaranteed to be in the pub if he needed company. He found a number that he'd very recently added to his phone and reluctantly called it, knowing his bills would double but, then, so would his fun.

"Tony?"

In truth, Bradley had always thought Tony was a bit of a loser. He'd never had a job, had no intention of finding work and no reason for being off. He was quite satisfied with spending every day in the Cross Keys, whereas Bradley considered himself to be between jobs, his last finishing the year before.

Tony drank very little while he was at the pub, unless someone else was around to pay his bar bill for him. However, while he was well known for being a bit of a leech, he always seemed harmless enough.

"Fancy a blast round the lake on a jet ski?"

There was no hesitation as the answer came back.

"Course I do, moneybags. Come and pick me up, yeah?"

Knowing he was in the pub, Bradley told Tony to keep it down. He didn't want everyone to know about his good fortune, an amount that was enough to keep him and Freya comfortable for a long while though not enough to spread around. Still, he figured he'd earned it and so wanted to have a little fun before he started looking at what they *needed* to spend it on.

An hour later, Bradley had eaten his breakfast and made his way to the pub to pick up his relatively new friend. The first thing Tony did was criticise the car, telling Bradley that he needed to trade it in and get something half decent.

"Won't that just advertise the fact that I've got money?"

Tony shook his head. "There's no point in having money if nobody knows about it. All those kids you went to school with, seeing you driving an old banger, will think you've done badly for yourself. Let 'em know, mate. You're big time now."

The kids at school were the last thing on his mind. He knew that a new car would give the game away to Freya and his fun would be over. That said, if he carried on with the car he had, he'd spend most of his fortune getting it repaired. Instead, another plan formed in his mind. He'd buy a modest new car and park it round the corner. Freya had said that Porsche Boxsters were quite cheap, considering how good they looked.

"Fine. Car first, then to the lake," he said, confirming it as he spoke.

The two of them drove to the nearby dealership that had sold Bradley his current car. He thought about his sadness at not being able to consult his wife, right up until the salesman brought out a shiny, three-year old, silver Porsche that had just been waxed.

"All yours for a deposit of ten percent, that's five thousand, seven hundred," he said casually.

Tony gasped. "That's a lot of car for fifteen grand, and it could be ours!"

"Excuse him," Bradley said, "Tony, it's fifty-seven grand."

His new friend shrugged, knowing it wasn't his either way.

"How much did you win, chief?"

Bradley kept his gaze on the car as he spoke. "Enough for this beauty. Can I put the deposit on a card?"

"Of course," the salesman replied, taking his card and walking swiftly into the office.

"You'll need a test drive, we insist," he concluded as he disappeared.

The deposit was taken from the card before the two customers left the showroom in the Porsche, Bradley driving while Tony pressed almost every button on the dashboard. He ran through the radio stations and other functions such as the media player, in awe at every moving part and shiny surround. The car had clearly been well looked after, though Bradley was more interested in the speeds he could achieve over the country roads. He had a near miss with a tractor, the farmer shaking his fist as Bradley blasted away, laughing as hard as Tony. The two of them made it back to the showroom and sorted the paperwork before zooming off for the last time, screaming in ecstasy at their newfound luxury.

Chapter 10

The Worst Day

Screeching tyres seemed to wake up the entire workshop as a car pulled up in front of the roller shutters and the customer burst out through the driver's door.

"Help!" was all she said as Freya looked up from under the car she was working on, noticed everyone else continuing to work, and finally stood to help the customer.

"Are you alright?" Freya asked, seeing the look of horror in the woman's eyes. "Can I help?"

Still tense, the customer spoke quickly about driving over a bump in the road that had caused a scraping sound and, being unsure of what the car looked like underneath, she'd driven straight to the garage to get it sorted. Freya nodded sympathetically, assuring the woman that it was common for speed bumps in particular to occasionally make contact with the car.

Freya put a jack under the car and lifted it, putting axle stands on either side before sliding underneath on a creeper.

"There it is," Freya said, pleased to find the issue straight away. "You've dinked the sump. It should be alright, but I'll take a proper look."

Freya came out from under the car, grabbed a nearby screwdriver and went back down. She gently scraped the sump to see if the crack looked particularly deep. All of a sudden, a gush of oil spilled from the hole and filled Freya's eye, leaving her blind and terrified. More oil gushed out and she panicked, trying to shield her face after dropping the screwdriver. Her workshop supervisor, Harry, saw the commotion and worried about the oil on the tarmac until he then realised that his apprentice was stuck beneath the car.

"Freya? Are you alright?"

He ran towards the car and pulled her legs, watching her emerge with a face full of thick, black oil. Her nose had started to fill, and her mouth was firmly closed to stop her from ingesting any more, leading her to suffocate in the shallow liquid. She felt the warm sun on her face and turned her head to allow the oil to slip off before blowing hard from her nose. Facing the floor, she screamed with a mixture of horror and relief, the concern for her eyesight still strong against the feeling of air finally filling her lungs.

Harry ran back to the workshop and grabbed a handful of rags, barking to a senior mechanic to call an ambulance. Freya could taste the old oil as she tried to spit it out, the rags finally taking the worst of the fluid from her face. Harry calmed her slightly, telling her that help was on the way and that she was out of danger, but she felt as humiliated as she was concerned for her health.

Within minutes, an ambulance pulled up to the garage and the paramedics wasted no time in getting her inside, the stress of the accident weighing heavily on her mind. Her face was cleaned as they made their way to hospital, the medics certain she'd need a doctor's attention. The journey was short and steady, the three of them making it to the hospital about the time that Freya's face was finally looking presentable.

It was an even shorter wait in Accident and Emergency, the department almost silent with the lack of patients. Freya was relieved to see so few in the waiting room, more so that she was wheeled straight into triage. Her shame was starting to overtake her panic, a good sign according to the doctor who saw her an hour after she'd arrived. He didn't seem concerned that she'd ingested much oil as she'd described keeping her mouth shut and controlling her breathing. He recommended taking the rest of the day off and she phoned Harry, who agreed that she should go home. He sounded relieved on the phone and it felt good to Freya that he'd been so sympathetic, expecting a round of abuse and taunting. She knew that would come the next day from the other lads, though she was getting used to that. As the only female mechanic in the garage, Freya had to work twice as hard to earn the smallest modicum of respect and there was always someone on hand to jeer her failures. Thick skin was entirely mandatory and could only be earned on the shop floor.

Getting out of the hospital was a nightmare as Freya didn't have enough for a taxi and had no idea where the bus stop was, deciding instead to call Bradley to pick her up. When he failed to answer, she had to call her supervisor for a lift.

"Where's that useless husband of yours?" Harry said as he pulled up, chuckling with a mischievous look on his face.

Freya was in no mood for joviality, cursing Bradley for his absence.

"He's not even looking for a job, he called in sick. Normally that means he's at home in his pants playing on his PlayStation. I bet he's just ignoring the phone."

"He looks more like an Xbox man to me," Harry said, avoiding her gaze as he tried to determine whether he'd gotten away with his comment.

That was before he realised that giving her a free lift entitled him to any amount of derogatory conversation, as long as it was about Bradley.

Freya huffed as she closed the passenger door behind her. "I wouldn't know the difference. Sorry about this."

She looked up to the sky, thinking about the different outcomes she'd avoided such as losing her eyesight or ingesting too much oil. Although she hid it well, she was thankful for the bearable nature of the accident.

Seeing how distraught Freya was, Harry told her not to worry, driving much slower than his usual manner to avoid her feeling sick. As they pulled up outside the house, Freya noticed that Bradley's car was missing. In no mood to play detective, she simply thanked Harry for the lift before making her way inside and to the bathroom to freshen up. The smell of oil particularly lingered in her hair and she was keen to get back to a bit of normality, soaking for over half an hour in the soothing, warm water.

There was still a distinct lack of her husband as she made her way to get dressed in the bedroom, choosing to get straight into pyjamas rather than put on a new outfit for the rest of the day. She was hoping he might have cooked for her, the taste of oil making her keen to eat something substantial. Admitting defeat, she put a tray of chips in the oven and made herself a sandwich while they cooked, coating the ham with tomato sauce in the hope that the viscosity would help it to remove the oil. Freya was pleased when the taste diminished and coated her chips with more ketchup to combat the last remnants of the wretched black substance. With her stomach full and an old film showing on the TV, she eventually drifted off to sleep, her concern for Bradley's whereabouts quickly fading away.

Chapter 11

Treading Water

As Freya was suffocating beneath a stranger's car, Bradley and Tony were pulling up by the coast in his brand-new convertible. He stroked the soft leather on the steering wheel as he rounded every corner and wondered why his newfound fortune hadn't come sooner.

"This is the place," Tony shouted as he jumped onto the seat and over the door to get out.

"Don't do that, mate. I haven't had it five minutes," Bradley whined, looking through sorrowful eyes.

Shaking his head, Tony told him he could just get another one the next day as he started to stroll along the rocky car park. He had gone to school with the owner of Southwest Jet Skis, Nathan, and had often talked about having a go—although his friend had known Tony's reputation and would never have let him ride for free. As they pulled up, Nathan clocked his old schoolmate and his whole body tensed. They'd had the conversation a thousand times before, though it looked as though he may have been ready to buckle.

"Don't worry," Tony said to Nathan, "We've got cash. Plenty of it."

A family was being served at the same time and their ears pricked up at the mere mention of wealth. Tony was smiling like a millionaire even though his clothes were way off the mark and Bradley was still feeling anxious in his company.

"Not plenty. Enough," Bradley said, giving his pal a playful tap on the arm.

Tony grinned widely. "Loads. In fact, mate, we'll pay for your family, too. We're minted."

As expected, the family took up the offer and Bradley found himself paying over twice the going rate for a ride on the jet skis as well as having to wait for them to finish. He pulled his friend to the side for a quiet word.

"Tony, *we're* not minted. *I* am, but if you carry on like this, there won't be anything for us to spend tomorrow."

"What?" Tony laughed. "Six hundred grand, mate. There might even be enough for the day after too."

Beside them, the wife giggled and congratulated Bradley on his money. They'd all looked when the Porsche had pulled up and looked more closely when two scruffy lads jumped out, yet the situation had concluded beautifully. Bradley thanked the woman humbly, letting them get on to the jet skis and taking a seat to wait until they'd all finished.

Having so much time sat doing nothing gave Tony an idea.

"Why are we renting these things when we could buy our own and spend all day down here?"

A motor started up nearby as Bradley shrugged his shoulders.

"How often are we going to be doing this?"

"Why does that matter? Let's get our own and get back down here."

He raised his voice for his other friend.

"Nathan, mate, we'll be back in a bit."

As Tony spoke, Nathan was still instructing the family on the safety of their vehicles, but he put a hand up and watched the two of them stroll away from the beach, Bradley's face contorted in disbelief as he reluctantly went along with the scheme. Half an hour later, they returned in a brand new Transit van with a spotless trailer carrying two gleaming jet skis.

Bounding out of the van like a puppy, Tony shouted for

Bradley. "Get these bad boys in the water!"

Bradley rolled his eyes and jumped out of the van, making for the trailer while Tony spoke to Nathan. He'd parked at the top of a hill that had a flat path cut into it, perfect for rolling the trailer straight into the sea. Upon purchase, the salesman had two young employees load the trailer up, meaning Bradley hadn't been used to the weight of it. As he unhooked it, the trailer took on a mind of its own and rolled down the hill, straight into the shallow water with a huge splash. As the trailer itself was fairly light, the buoyancy of the jet skis kept it afloat and Tony finally sprang into action, untying their new toys ready for their first ride.

Nathan was concerned watching the two of them.

"Do you know how to handle those? Did you even buy wetsuits?"

Tony laughed and Bradley shrugged.

"How hard can it be?"

They jumped on in their soaking clothes, figuring the heat of the day would dry them off eventually and started them up as they'd been instructed.

Watching in despair, Nathan tried to keep an eye on them as well as the family he was serving. Bradley was having the time of his life, however. He'd only been in the sea as a child, yet owned the waves as an adult on a luxury he never considered he even wanted. He thought about Freya, although mostly about how much trouble he'd be in if she ever found out. He constructed a mundane lie for where he'd been during the day as he chased Tony around the bay, loving the feeling of the water gently splashing his face.

Having even more fun was Tony, who couldn't hide his surprise at his sudden access to a fortune. He rounded rocks and crashed through the small waves with the biggest smile Bradley had ever seen, any regard for the condition of his ride completely diminished. He avoided crashing it yet scraped it along the obstacles, showing absolutely no remorse.

Bradley was much more careful with his, realising that

luck was the only reason he had one in the first place. They both ventured outside the bay briefly but came back almost instantly, realising they'd have no chance if either of them fell in. The sea tended to be where families from their town went rather than drunkards like them and Bradley felt temporarily out of place.

It took around an hour before they both got bored and decided to make their way back in. Bradley was particularly hungry, the adrenaline of nearly losing two jet skis adding to his emptiness. Tony suggested burgers, yet Bradley knew that they had access to much better places. He'd have to dress them, as waterlogged jeans and T-shirts would never have gone down well at the Seafront Hotel, and so they loaded up the trailer and made their way to a suitable tailor before dining on a five course meal.

As their waiter brought each plate out, both men frowned at the size of the portions. Despite the number of courses, the amount of food was certainly less than they'd imagined. Tony had turned his nose up at the thought of goat's cheese parcels, but was wishing for more once he'd devoured the two small slices. Soup bowls were delivered as their second course, which managed to last for two literal swigs before they were gone, both lads drinking from their bowls and leaving the cutlery where it was to the disgust of other patrons. They'd both opted for the seafood surprise as a main, and the same theme continued through their entire conversation.

"The biggest surprise here is the lack of stuff to eat," Tony loudly declared.

By the time Bradley pushed the final prawn into his mouth, both had disregarded thoughts of a massive dessert. They were proven correct, and couldn't even make up for it on their final cheese and cracker course. As both stood up to leave, they looked like they'd been thrown out, such was the ire etched onto their faces after finally receiving an eye-watering bill.

"I'm still hungry, let's grab a pizza," Tony was heard to say as he left the exclusive restaurant, Bradley also feeling unfulfilled.

Chapter 12

Under The Influence

Clunk. The sound of the front door woke Freya from her slumber and she looked straight towards it to see her husband swaying and grinning. From his expression, he'd clearly spent yet another day with Tony from the Cross Keys though she didn't want to immediately accuse him.

"Where's the car?" she asked as an ice breaker.

Without so much as a pause, Bradley burst into hysterics.

"It's round the corner so Freya doesn't find out... Oops, you're Freya!" he said, falling to the floor as the laughter took hold of his body.

"It had better be in one piece."

She was in no mood to worry about the damage she would potentially be repairing over the next week. Instead, she stood up and walked over to him, showing her disdain with a single look. She folded her arms and watched as his hilarity subsided.

Bradley looked up from the floor and caught Freya's eye, realising that he was probably in more trouble than he'd imagined. He let out a final chuckle and wobbled back to his feet, asking if the two of them could sit down if she wanted to chat. Keen to get details of his impromptu day off without her, Freya agreed and they sat opposite each other on separate sides of the living room.

"A tea would be lovely," he slurred playfully.

He clearly knew that his chances of Freya providing such a service went out of the window several pints ago.

Freya simply nodded, clearly frustrated, and asked him if he'd been drinking with Tony at the pub all day. He looked up at the ceiling in contemplation and finally told her that he had and that the pub had called louder than the PlayStation that day. Freya nodded again, this time to show that she'd been correct in her prediction, and asked him how he was meant to look for work the next day if he was in that state. Another stare at the ceiling followed before Bradley smiled once more.

"I can't go anywhere, I think I'm still sick," he said before going to tap himself on the nose. He missed and ended up pointing towards the front door.

This made him laugh again, frustrating Freya even further.

"Do you know what happened to me at work today?"

The question made Bradley stop laughing and he shrugged, stopping to listen.

Freya went into detail about the sump emptying over her and how scared she'd been for her health, at one point feeling like she was going to drown.

"I couldn't even get hold of you to get a lift back and now I find out it's because you were drinking with *Tony* all day! You don't even like the bloke."

This made Bradley frown, apparently in thought, and he conceded almost immediately.

"Nah, not really. I mean, he's alright but... he's no, *you*."

Freya simmered at his response. "So why didn't you get me to take the day off so we could go drinking together? What am I saying? You knew I couldn't get the day off. The garage can't give me time off with that short notice."

"Exactly, I was thinking of you. Tony took a lager bullet for you. Actually, he took loads. Maybe he's not so bad."

The situation became more suspicious to Freya, although she put it down to him just wanting a day off. She was sure Tony just happened to be there and he was hard to shake, particularly if someone else was paying.

"You'd better cover the bills this month," she said, knowing there was little else she could really say.

He'd been out, got drunk and was back. Anything else was surely his problem, as long as they didn't end up on the street.

Although it had taken a while, Freya's story seemed to finally hit Bradley as he looked towards her with sad eyes.

"How are you now, Babe?"

He leant on his hand, which suddenly gave way beneath him, causing his head to drop and bounce off the arm of the chair. Freya laughed quietly, enjoying his pain just a little too much.

"I think I'm alright. Harry gave me a lift back."

As she spoke, Freya expected a little jealousy from her husband. Instead, she watched him close his eyes and nod firmly, swaying in the seat as he did so.

"Good, good. He's a nice chap, say thanks to you—him, for doing that for us later on today."

Bradley's incoherence suggested it was time for him to get to bed and Freya was feeling the effects of falling asleep on the sofa, her neck aching and her back stiff. She stood up and offered a peaceful hand to him.

"Let's go upstairs," she suggested.

With that, he stood, grabbed her hand and yanked himself up, almost pulling Freya's arm out of the socket. He sprang upright and opened his eyes wide, an 'uh oh' expression moulded to his features. Freya had seen that look a thousand times and yelled for him to run upstairs to the toilet, words that seemed to bounce off the side of his head as he ignored the instruction. He let out a tiny burp that sounded almost childlike, the precursor to a sea of vomit that exploded out of his mouth and onto the carpet in front of Freya. Her instinct was to jump back, which launched her over the sofa and on to the other side with a *thud*.

Bradley collapsed to the floor and, using the food and beer that he'd consumed as a pillow, started to drool.

"Time for Bradley's bedtime," he said as he closed his eyes and coughed.

The stench of the digested food hit Freya and she urged, knowing there was no way she'd be able to clean it up. Bradley looked in danger of drowning himself with the sheer amount he was lying in and Freya could have sworn she'd seen undigested prawns lying lifeless in the foul liquid. Work beckoned in the morning and Bradley was clearly looking at another day off so she pulled him to his feet, avoiding the drips that flew from his face, and ushered him upstairs.

Placing him in their bed after cleaning the worst of it off his face, Freya issued a stern warning not to throw up in their bed. He was clearly not receiving, having closed his eyes and drifted straight to sleep and so Freya slipped into the third of the bed she'd been left, ready for a terrible night's sleep worrying about her idiot husband.

Chapter 13

Place Your Bets

Bradley had woken feeling unusually fresh following so many sessions of drinking, although Freya suggested that he was probably still drunk from the night before. He shrugged, watched her go to work and then got dressed quickly. He noticed that Freya had stopped asking why he wasn't parking on the drive anymore, hoping he'd kept his cool enough for her to stop worrying.

The drive to Tony's was treacherous, to say the least, particularly considering that he only lived a few minutes away from the couple. Bradley suggested they take a day off from celebrating, noticing a glint in Tony's eye as he finished speaking.

"Or," Tony said without a pause, "we could get suited and booted before making our way to Bristol."

Bradley frowned. "Bristol? What's so interesting there?"

A manic grin ripped its way across Tony's face.

"Casinos!"

The word struck Bradley as a little odd. He'd already won a ton of money, why would he want to gamble it all away?

Tony, as ever, had the answer.

"Mate, you know yourself that Bigbet was a goldmine if you had enough to put on a dead cert. A pound on a guaranteed horse got you a few extra pence, but a thousand pounds on the same horse at least paid for your beer. Let's take a grand each and see if we can win big... again!"

The cogs were turning in his friend's mind, but the alcohol was starting to win. Bradley had envisaged a day off falling asleep and catching up, although he figured that a trip to Bristol could be a way of compromising.

"Let's take the train though, I'm too hammered to drive. I nearly killed Felix Weir's little sister on the way over."

They both stood in silence for a long minute to think about Felix Weir's little sister, particularly how she'd grown from a vicious, sarcastic schoolkid and blossomed into adulthood, becoming a magazine regular who littered her social media with modelling photos. Bradley had to snap them out of it.

"So, the train. We'll grab the next one to Bristol, get threaded up and spend a maximum of a grand at the casinos to beat them."

"We'll need a grand each, but yeah, good plan."

The most important part of the plan was sleep, but while Bradley thought it, he'd never have said it.

Ten minutes later, they walked to the crowded station to find their train would arrive in another fifteen. Bradley grumbled, grabbing a couple of chocolate bars for his breakfast and hoping he could stay upright for that long. Tony didn't seem in such a poor state, although Bradley figured this was probably because drinking was his career. Leaves on the line meant an extra ten minutes before the train actually arrived and Bradley was in a foul mood as the carriages finally trickled to a stop beside them.

"Come on, grumpy. I thought we were going to have a great day," Tony said jovially.

This just made his new pal want to hit him even more.

They made their way to a table, realising that a couple was already at the first before turning to look for a clear one. The seats behind them were filling fast and so they jumped onto the remaining two by the table and smiled at the couple who simply nodded in return. There was no chance Bradley was going to fall asleep in front of a pair of strangers and so he committed to their day out instead, trying to sober up as the train marched on.

He felt much better once they'd pulled into Bristol station and the two of them made their way to the nearest tailor, using the map app to guide them.

"We look mint, mate!" Tony said to Bradley, the tailor rolling his eyes as though such expressions were never used in his establishment.

This went completely unnoticed by the pair who were getting excited at the prospect of winning some extra funds in their new tuxedos, although Bradley was sure that Tony would claim any winnings as his own.

The casino was buzzing when they got there with tourists carrying around cups of change as they'd seen so often in films set in Las Vegas. They were keen for the table games, though, buying a thousand pounds worth of chips on Bradley's credit card. Both started cautiously, watching their funds slip away pound by pound on the roulette table. Tony finally managed to win one round and loudly declared that he was on a roll, placing half of his remaining pot on 35. When 17 came up, he told Bradley that 35 was slightly bolder on the table and put the remaining pot on there again to lose it to 7.

"You know what we need? More chips!" Tony declared.

Bradley felt a sickness in his stomach.

"We've already blown two grand!"

Tony tutted. "Yeah, out of six hundred. We've barely scratched the surface."

"My card won't go much higher, mate. I have no idea what's left on it."

Without a pause, the roulette dealer intervened. He told the pair that the casino owner was happy to provide credit and would even put betting limits on to make sure they didn't exceed their budget. Tony was petulantly goading Bradley, particularly as they'd dressed to impress yet spent less than twenty minutes in the casino. Bradley reluctantly agreed, knowing he still had plenty of cash to come. His Bigbet winnings hadn't yet been paid, though he still had the confirmation on his phone and the casino owner was willing to take it as proof of his worth.

Another two thousand chips were issued yet, this time, they only lasted ten minutes.

"What the hell, Tony?"

Bradley noticed that his companion had absolutely no control and was throwing chips onto tables seemingly at random. They'd blown four thousand between them and yet Tony was back with the manager, asking for more.

In all, they spent four hours at the casino and Tony's bets were getting bigger and bigger as he chased their losses. Bradley thought he'd kept track at the beginning, although on leaving, he realised that a lot of bets had been completely forgotten.

"We've burnt nearly a hundred grand!" Bradley said, the sick feeling in his stomach intensifying as his hangover reappeared with gusto. "What were you thinking?"

Tony was wide eyed and apparently remorseful, biting his bottom lip as he came to terms with their day in Bristol. His weak apology spilled out as they walked, bewildered, from the casino.

"At least you've still got half a million left..." he added.

The truth didn't help Bradley at all. Losing a sixth of his winnings without a single memento of their visit cut through him immensely.

"I nicked a chip," Tony said unhelpfully, tossing a pound's worth of plastic towards his friend.

Bradley sighed.

"Perhaps we can build back from this to a hundred grand."

He put the chip in his pocket, and they made their way back to the station, making no plans to meet that evening.

Chapter 14

Freya's Turn

"Fancy dress party?"

By the time Freya made it home from work, Bradley was asleep on the sofa in his new tuxedo. He looked up at his wife with ultra-sad eyes, although she found it hard to give him sympathy.

"This old thing?" he said, the usual charm completely absent from his words.

His skin was pale and he looked ill, though Freya knew it was most likely through drinking so much.

"I'm out tonight, look after the place. I'm going to be late," Freya said abruptly.

Although she was only half joking when she replied, the thought of a night out with her friends became more appealing as she considered her own suggestion. Putting her bag down, she pulled her phone out and sent a message to three of her closest friends.

Watching her through half closed eyes, Bradley frowned with sorrow.

"Can't you keep me company? I've had a terrible day," he said without elaborating any further.

Freya stopped what she was doing and slowly turned her head to look at him.

"Are you kidding? You've been on a bender all weekend, taken two days off job searching when you're struggling to pay your bills and now you want me to stay home because you're a little bit hungover? Absolutely not!"

As she spoke, her phone vibrated and she checked the

message, a confirmation from the first of her friends. The other two, Darlene and her colleague, Sheila, had also both messaged to say they were unavailable, although Freya was happy to be going out with just one of them.

Lifting the top of his body from the sofa, Bradley tried to look hurt that his wife was abandoning him.

"What time will you be back?"

All she could offer in return was a quick, "very late," before she ascended the stairs and got changed and ready for the evening.

She wasn't planning on getting too drunk as she knew work awaited the next morning, yet it was rare she was in the mood for a night out at the Cross Keys. Half an hour later, the doorbell rang, although Freya could hear that Bradley was in no rush to answer it.

"Down in a second," she called, hoping he'd take the hint and get up.

Eventually, he did.

Standing in front of him was Kayla, Freya's best friend since they were in primary school together. They'd been inseparable throughout school and college, although their work lives had meant they'd seen a lot less of each other. Kayla's personality was the exact opposite of Freya's, her extroverted nature leading them into verbal altercations on regular occasions. Although she scolded her friend afterwards, Freya enjoyed the feeling of being animated and asserting herself from time to time, even if it didn't come naturally to her.

"Fancy dress party?" Kayla asked as Bradley answered the door. Freya knew they were in for a good night.

The walk to the pub involved catching up, as Freya told Kayla about Bradley's odd behaviour and saved the mystery of the missing car until last. Kayla was single at that point, having dumped her last boyfriend for trying to propose in a restaurant. She'd found the ring that had been meant for her and told him that she wasn't ready to be tied down, to which he'd sulked and then left. Freya laughed at the image. She'd enjoyed being married to Bradley as he often found them exciting things to do at the weekend, yet his recent behaviour had worn thin.

As they went through the front door, Freya couldn't believe what she was seeing. There at the bar was Tony in an identical tuxedo to Bradley, although he had a blue shirt on instead of white.

"He's been with his boyfriend all day," Freya said to Kayla, never taking her eyes off Tony.

He seemed to be having the time of his life, standing at the end of the bar and repeatedly lifting his drink in the air. He was making engine noises over and over, his circle of drinking partners laughing loudly every time he did. Freya tried to ignore him, getting a round in and retiring to a nearby table to catch up with Kayla some more.

After half an hour, an older gentleman walked past and nodded to Freya.

"Well done, lass. He's a lucky bugger, I'n't 'e?"

Freya nodded, smiling as she did so and then shooting Kayla a confused look. She didn't think anything of it. Instead, she told her old pal how she'd covered her entire head in oil, Kayla choosing to laugh hysterically rather than offer any sympathy. This made Freya chuckle, although she blocked out the worst of the memories from the day before.

Gin was the drink of the night as the pair got through more glasses than intended. Freya started to worry about whether she'd make it in to work the next day. Calling in sick wasn't an option as two of her workmates passed through the Cross Keys that night and saw her drinking with a friend, both saying a brief hello as they passed. As an apprentice, she worried that her boss would never forgive her for taking the day off at such short notice and started to hope that she'd feel well enough to at least work the day and get to bed early.

Kayla noticed her concerned look growing more evident and asked if she was alright, to which Freya could only bring herself back to the room and nod enthusiastically. She was enjoying herself overall and certain that Bradley would be missing her, a fitting revenge.

Midnight came and Freya knew that she had to call time on their night out, suggesting a kebab before they both made their way home. Kayla invited Freya to stay with her, although they both knew that the night would never end if they both went back to the same house.

The kebab shop was empty when they arrived, although the staff were priming themselves for the rush that was sure to follow once the pubs all called time on their patrons. Freya thought about getting Bradley something, even just as a thank you for her new ring, before finally deciding that he'd been out all day and bought himself a ridiculously expensive suit without buying her so much as a bag of crisps. She looked down at her new ring, connecting the price of the jewellery with the suit as she saw them in her mind. Was he as lucky as the passing stranger had insinuated?

Chapter 15

The Return Of Skeleton Crew

The room was spinning around Bradley.

He couldn't believe he'd allowed Tony to take him for a hundred grand, kicking himself harder when he realised his own part. Every positive thought was pushed out of his mind by the lost money, a sum he'd not actually been paid at that point. He still had his credit card, though, and so he figured he could probably make a couple of thousand back at Bigbet with a few taps of his phone.

It was an investment, he told himself.

He logged on, seeing the usual array of flashing images and scantily clad models designed to entice him into staying on the site.

Skeleton Crew was the only game he had any knowledge of, and he found himself back there without much thought. His account was showing as empty, causing the cashier to flash up.

Did he want to make a deposit?

Of course, he thought, entering the card details and watching two thousand pounds flash up in his account.

"Let's see if we can double that, shall we?" he said to himself, tapping the button to spin the reels for a pound a bet.

Symbols came and went as he robotically clicked the screen, wondering why such a simple game could be so addictive. He watched the numbers on the monster jackpot creeping up, remembering that first surge of euphoria when he realised he'd won previously. That was so far removed from how he was feeling just a few days later, a significant chunk of his winnings spent without any reward. The casino had sent him a reminder email about the amount he owed, and attached, were penalties for non-payment, which spiralled into further thousands of pounds. He was confident he could get the amount paid back, although the threat was enough to make him nervous.

This was all playing on his mind as he went through several bonus rounds, never winning more than a hundred pounds at a time. That gave him enough to simply keep spinning as he vowed not to remove less than four thousand from his account, a system that saw his initial deposit dwindle before midnight hit.

He felt a huge void within him, crushing his organs and adding to his stress. He always imagined being rich to be freeing, yet he felt the loss of his money more strongly than any other feeling he'd experienced. Pressing 'Deposit' again, he was stunned to see a 'card declined' message on the site. Sweat was pouring out of him as his heart rate increased, hardly believing what he was seeing. How much had he spent altogether? He knew it wasn't everything, yet the casino bill had knocked him, and he knew the card limit was high at twelve thousand pounds. Could it be right?

In his mind, there was only one way to check and he went to his normal online shop, browsing for DVD box sets that totalled over a thousand pounds. He slowly decreased the number every time his card was rejected, finally getting the total to a hundred pounds.

"What the..?"

Bradley put his head in his hands, cursing himself for not keeping tabs on his expenditure. The nights at the bar, the Porsche deposit, the jet skis... A quick note on the prices would have given him some idea of what he'd been throwing around.

He started to regret agreeing to pay for drinks and meals, more so when he thought of Tony hanging beside him, telling others of his wealth and inviting them in. Worse still, Freya knew nothing about it. He knew he should have alerted her, even if it was just to set them up for life. He closed the shopping app, went back to Bigbet and double checked his balance.

£0.00.

With no credit card, he was effectively broke and couldn't even cheer himself up with a pizza. He checked the fridge, finding very little on the shelves that weren't either a condiment or sandwich filling. There was no bread, meaning his choice of soggy lettuce—which technically belonged to Freya—accompanied by mayonnaise, mint sauce or tomato paste didn't seem particularly appealing. He thought of calling Tony, asking him to get something hot from town, before realising that he'd have to pay for it and then indulge in more of Tony's deepest desires. At that time of night, he rarely thought of anything above the waist. He imagined Freya coming home to a couple of sex workers, both bought for Tony, telling him that they still had time on the clock. She'd never have believed his innocence.

His next thought rocked him completely. Were Bigbet completely committed to paying out? Did he have any protection if they decided it was a glitch on the website?

He sprang his phone back to life, searching forums for bookies who'd gone back on their promise to pay their customers. Most were for general betting, where odds had changed and the company wasn't liable for their errors, yet he realised that he still may never see the money.

Going into his emails, he stared at the confirmation from the company and looked for a follow up, finding nothing else to suggest the payout wouldn't happen. His paranoia increased tenfold having seen the comments, however. He felt like he was losing his mind. The only solution was distraction, and so he found a film and hoped it would drown out the savage voices.

The success was noted an hour later when he was deep into the story, Freya's wobbling silhouette in the hallway finally pulling him back to reality. Bradley could see that she had a kebab and started to drool, wiping his chin before his wife could see him. Fortunately, she was failing to remove her shoes, swaying as she bent down for them and almost dropping her snack as she did so. Bradley dove forward to help out, guiding her to the bottom of the stairs and allowing her to sit back while he did the work. Freya had a mouthful of kebab and was breathing heavily through it, the smell both horrifying but disturbingly inviting. He knew that his own portion of it would taste sublime against his empty stomach, trying to put hunger out of his mind.

Freya mumbled that she loved him, never really looking his way as she did so. Her eyes opened and closed slowly, every bite seeming to zap her energy as she chewed. Free from her shoes, she leant forward and kissed Bradley on the forehead, telling him she had to work the next day. She smiled manically, making him wonder if she'd actually make it before watching her take herself up to bed. He promised to follow her up, deciding instead to finish his film. He also noticed that Freya had left half of her kebab and was unable to stop himself from finishing that, too.

Chapter 16

A Big Deposit

Freya's revenge almost turned into empathy as she woke up to a spinning room. Her late night catching up with an old friend almost instantly became a regret as the alarm buzzed beside her. Bradley grunted and rolled over, leaving Freya to make her way to the bathroom to throw up in the toilet before deciding how she was going to make it through a whole day at work in her condition.

After getting dressed and wobbling towards the bedroom door, Freya had the feeling she'd left her phone on the bedside table and knew she couldn't leave the house without checking it. Kayla was likely to have put pictures of their night out online, which, coupled with the fact they'd been spotted, meant she definitely couldn't phone in sick. However, she also checked her bank account every morning to make sure no surprises lay in store. She grabbed her phone and fumbled down the stairs, keeping hold of the banister as she went for fear of plunging headfirst down the flight.

Breakfast was out since she could still taste the chunks of second-hand kebab between her teeth and so she made a coffee instead, dropping three sugars into it where she normally took none. The sweetness coursed over her tongue and Freya indulged in the feeling, the only positive vibe she'd had since waking.

Focusing hard on the screen in front of her, she fired her phone into life and went straight to her messages where, sure enough, notifications alerted her to Kayla's busy night after they'd parted. Not wanting to see several photos of her in various states,

Freya instead went to her banking app and checked in to their joint current account.

She knew she was seeing double when the balance came up as it looked like they had six hundred thousand pounds in their joint account, and so she took another hit of coffee and rubbed her eyes to get the sleep out. She then returned to her phone and saw the same figure, next believing it to be a bank error.

£642,105.61, consisting of her balance the previous night of £113.25 to roughly cover three bills that were due to go and a payment of £641,992.36 from a company she'd never heard of. Her stomach was doing somersaults as she imagined the company finding their mistake and removing the money later in the day and she figured she could borrow it for a couple of days, maybe even a week, to get the interest from having such a huge sum in her personal savings account.

With the push of a few buttons, she transferred the big payment realising that Bradley would likely have some questions yet putting that out of her mind for the time being.

The money had distracted Freya for longer than she had to spare and, with a headache to boot, she knew that driving wasn't an option. Vowing to explain her entire situation to Harry when she arrived, Freya phoned him quickly to say that she would be late and apologised without giving any information. She then walked out of the front door and made her way to the garage, imagining that she could keep the money and deciding what she would do with such an amount. Would she go fifty-fifty with Bradley, or would he allow her to pay their mortgage along with some bills and then split the money to enjoy whatever remained?

The fresh air was helping her hangover to recede, although she wondered how much of the spring in her step could be attributed to the feeling of being wealthy for the first time in her life. A smile passed over her mouth, although she knew how dangerous the promise of money that wasn't actually available could be. Putting it out of her mind seemed the only sensible thing to do as the disappointment of losing it was bound to be at least as heavy as her happiness was. Instead, she thought about the workload that was waiting for her at the garage.

Pulling up to the front door, Harry was waiting for her with a serious expression on his face. Freya shouted an apology as soon as she knew he could hear her, yet he simply gestured towards his office and started walking in. As she sat in the chair in front of his desk, she tripped over her words in a bid to get them out quickly, telling him that she couldn't afford to lose her job and that she would never be late again.

Harry shook his head and simply replied with, "Phone for you. I think it's Bradley," before he sat back in his seat, waiting for her response.

Frowning as she picked up the phone, Freya wondered what her boss was thinking.

"Hello?" she said nervously.

"You! Where's my money, bitch?"

Freya could hardly believe what she was hearing. Bradley had never spoken to her in that way and had always been quite sweet, even when he was drunk. From his voice, she could tell that he was angry and his tone was that of a loan shark who'd given his client enough time to pay him back. The change in him was hard to accept and Freya's stomach cramped as she started to realise what had happened.

"*Your* money? Where did you get it from? You've got to deal drugs or win the lottery to get that much paid into your—our—account!"

Freya was careful not to anger him further, even though she felt he had a case to answer.

Still, he refused. Instead, Bradley just repeated his question in a more direct manner, but without the name calling.

Neither had ever resorted to it in the past and this made Freya sure that the money had been acquired illegally.

"Let's talk about it face to face," she offered, turning to

face Harry to get him on her side.

She was already late, yet she wanted him to be sure that it wasn't entirely her fault.

"If that's what you want. I'm coming down there," Bradley said calmly before hanging up.

Freya quickly looked at her phone to confirm that the call had ended and went pale, her legs weakening beneath her.

"He's coming here," she said to Harry, the horror evident on her face.

Freya imagined what Bradley might do or say when he showed up, the wait proving to be torture until he arrived.

Chapter 17

The Realisation

After seeing Freya leaving for work, Bradley had gone back to sleep briefly before he was woken by a vivid dream of Tony driving his Porsche into the sea where they'd launched the jet skis. He rubbed his eyes and yawned, grabbing his phone as he did so to see if his winnings had been paid in. It was becoming a bit of a ritual and he was certain that, if the money never arrived, he'd still look for it first thing every day.

Normally, he only checked his solo account as he and Freya had both set up accounts for their own purchases. After noticing it was still almost completely empty, a nagging doubt entered his mind and he decided to check the joint account that their benefits and Freya's salary were paid into before they split the remaining cash between them. Although the balance was once again low, he looked through the transactions and saw that the payment from Bigbet had gone in, almost immediately followed by a slightly larger withdrawal. His face dropped and an army of butterflies worked hard within his stomach.

We've been hacked! he thought, rubbing his cheek in a bid to calm his nerves.

The tension within him was rising exponentially as he tried to work out how he'd get the money back, if indeed it hadn't been paid out and retracted by Bigbet themselves. There was no way to contact them by phone, yet he found an email address for their customer service department and rapidly fired a message their way to see what had happened. Next, he picked up his phone to call Tony.

The phone was answered within a couple of rings and his new friend seemed very jovial, even for him.

"Hey, pal! What are we up to today?"

Bradley closed his eyes and rubbed them, trying to think of what to say without giving the game away.

"Are you paying today?" was all he could think of.

Tony was quiet at the other end, making Bradley suspicious for a second.

Finally, he replied with, "Mate, I'm really sorry. I thought you were sharing your big win. I wasn't trying to take advantage. You know I couldn't afford to repay you. We spent a bucket load just at the casino yesterday. I can grab you a packet of pork scratchings and head over if you like?"

Everything about the call made sense. His apologetic tone, his realisation, right down to the fact he was keen to get straight over and start another day. If he'd stolen the money, Bradley was sure he'd be long gone by now. He sighed, keeping the receiver by his mouth, and his next suspect came into view in his mind.

"The money's gone. It's been stolen from my account."

Further silence ensued, followed by Tony sounding more than a little confused.

"What? It can't have been. Surely nobody had enough time. Come on, someone hacked your account on the very day you got your big win paid to you?"

"Freya?"

Tony sucked in as much air as would fill his lungs, the sound of its release almost deafening in Bradley's ear.

"No! Did you tell her about it? How did she get into your account?"

Concern for where Freya may have actually gone started to pulsate in Bradley's mind. With that amount, she could well have left the country, although he was sure she couldn't have checked into an airport and flown within that time.

Bradley looked up at the ceiling, cursing his idiocy for keeping the wrong bank details tied to his Bigbet account. He'd treated his weekend flutters as a shared expense, always watching money going into the account from his debit card, but never actually having to retrieve anything following his multiple losses. He realised why it was important to double check these things now and again, especially where the potential for big wins was present.

"It went into the joint account. She must have transferred it into her own savings account. I guess Bigbet had our joint details."

"Ah, that was dumb," came the reply, which did nothing to alleviate Bradley's concerns. "Mate, the world was meant to be our oyster. We were finally beginning to enjoy life; it has nothing to do with her. Get it back!"

Tony was speaking so quickly that the words were battering Bradley's ear. This annoyed him further, to the point that he almost blew.

"What do you think I'm going to do, Tony? Leave it go? Hope she brings it back? Your constant moaning isn't going to help. Besides, it's my money, not ours. When did you become my personal charity case?"

"When you realised you're no fun on your own, I guess."

The reply was curt and cutting, although Bradley was certain he'd have been bored to tears walking around a casino on his own. That said, he would probably have almost all of his money left. Tony's speed of reply stopped him from registering this last thought, however.

"Mate, get off the phone to me and get hold of her. Maybe it was a mistake, but she has no right to it. If the taxman gets nothing, and he can put you in jail, I see no reason why your selfish wife can throw it on clothes and shoes... or shack up with another bloke."

Bradley couldn't take the thought of his wife leaving him or spending all his new fortune and so he simply said, "I'll bell you back," and disconnected the call.

He checked the bank once more and noticed that the payment reference for the transfer was blank, meaning it had likely been withheld. He had no proof that Freya had the cash, although everything he'd discussed with Tony had made perfect sense. She was awake, out of the house, and had direct access to their account. His only shot was to phone her, realising that she'd probably never answer her mobile if she had taken the money. Instead, he decided to call her supervisor to make sure he had a witness to the scandalous way he'd been treated.

He'd never called his wife anything other than cute nicknames, though he started to imagine that Harry may well have been in on her deceit. Perhaps he'd been seducing her all along, waiting for the right opportunity to snatch her from Bradley. This sent him over the edge and, when Harry answered, he was seething with rage. Hearing that Freya had pulled up to the garage, he couldn't help but unleash his fury. The next step was to get the money back and get his new credit paid off.

Chapter 18
The Big Reveal

Harry was watching the window after Bradley's call, clearly waiting for him to turn up so he could spring into action. Freya was in bits, her mind racing as she tried to imagine every outcome of his visit. He'd never been close to violence in the past, his hostile tone the absolute peak of his aggression in their time together. However, her most disturbing thought was that he'd never called her a bitch before. Freya knew all too well that money changed people although, in her experience, it was normally a lack of funds that made people desperate and selfish. She never imagined for a minute that a six-figure pay out would turn her mischievous yet loving husband into such a monster.

After a coffee, Freya sat on the sofa in Harry's office and breathed deeply to settle her nerves. The silence was unbearable, and so she replayed her version of events to Harry, reminding him that she'd had no idea where the money came from.

Harry put his head to one side in thought.

"There must be a legitimate reason for him receiving such a specific amount, right down to the 36 pence. Why did you transfer it in the first place?"

Explaining her panic, Freya told him about her plan to pay it back slowly and make a bit of money on the interest, to which he shook his head and sighed. He told her that even a high amount of money would have yielded a small amount of interest in her account and that the company would have known she couldn't spend it all in a day, meaning she'd have been forced to give it straight back. Freya nodded, understanding his point and admitting it was only a fleeting idea. By then, she was more concerned about her husband's reaction, figuring that giving the money back to the company was his problem unless it was legitimately his to keep.

As she finished her sentence, a commotion occurred in the salesroom below and Freya knew that Bradley had arrived. He confirmed it by shouting at the receptionist, after which Harry barrelled down the stairs to intervene.

"Ah, there he is. Where's Freya?" Bradley asked abruptly.

He was breathing heavily, his blinkered focus obvious to the crowd that was starting to surround him. Harry advised him to calm down and led him up the stairs, talking loudly so that Freya would know to hide. She'd been watching from the top of the stairs and immediately disappeared from view as she heard the first footstep at the bottom of the flight.

Harry sat Bradley down and gave him a coffee, the years of customer service evident to those present. They started to talk about Bradley's intentions and he was honest about the money, telling Harry that it belonged to him and he wanted it back. Harry made him promise to remain calm and then offered to bring out Freya, who remained hidden until she could see he was unlikely to cause any harm.

The situation was far removed from anything that Freya was expecting to come up against in her lifetime and she sat across from Bradley, looking at him cautiously with every movement. Harry perched on the end of the sofa, close to his worker in case of an escalation. Her first question was inevitable.

"Where did the money come from, Bradley?"

Sucking in a lungful of air, Bradley took his time to respond.

"I won it on Saturday; it was the monster jackpot on Bigbet. I stuck a fiver on Skeleton Crew and it came in."

Before he'd finished speaking, Harry interrupted. "Skeleton Crew? Is that the name of a horse? You know gambling's for mugs, don't you, mate?"

Jarring his head to the left, Bradley looked straight into Harry's eyes and shot him a warning glance. Freya asked Harry not to speak as she wanted to know the whole story, figuring there must have been more given the amount of time he had to spend his winnings. It certainly explained why he'd bought new clothes, although the disappearance of the car was still weighing heavily on her mind. Fortunately, she didn't have to ask.

"The car's gone. I swapped it for a Porsche."

This revelation made Harry laugh sarcastically and he stared at Bradley with an aggressively smug look. Freya once more asked him to stay out of it, although she was pleased to have his presence as it made her feel safe.

"That was my car you swapped. Where's the Porsche?"

Looking at the floor, Bradley started to piece together their time apart.

"I parked it around the corner so you wouldn't see it. Currently, it's at Tony's. You know all about my drinking this weekend. You probably don't know about the jet skis and the day in the casino. I've spent..." he thought for a minute, still looking at the floor, "quite a bit, actually. Now they want it back."

In an instant, Harry lunged at Bradley and grabbed his head, locking his arm and dragging him from the sofa. Bradley tried to resist, pulling his head backwards and shouting for Harry to leave him alone. Freya stood up and joined in the shouting, almost going to separate them yet realising that Harry was most likely to catch her accidentally if she tried. Finally, she said something that brought his sense back.

"It was his money he was spending. It has nothing to do with either of us!"

The revelation stopped the commotion in an instant and Harry let go of Bradley, who shoved him in return. Harry laughed at the ineffectiveness of the gesture, and went to stand by Freya, again making her feel safe.

"I just want to know why you felt you didn't want to share it?"

The question lay heavy in the air until Bradley was ready to answer.

"At first, I wanted to enjoy it. I've never had that much to play with. It just got out of control; I didn't keep any kind of track on it and yesterday was a real eye opener to how quickly it could be spent, especially when you're paying for another person's happiness."

He rolled his eyes following the last sentence, knowing how stupid it sounded.

"Tony?" Freya asked, knowing the answer deep down.

Bradley explained that it wasn't just Tony. The whole pub had helped him to celebrate on that first night and they'd given money away to strangers in the casino, mostly to pay for their food.

Freya rubbed her eyes and looked to the ceiling.

"And you didn't want me there? Where the hell do we go from here?"

A cold silence dropped around them as Freya waited for Bradley to answer. She tried to imagine her life from here, a sliding doors moment where her only real choice was to keep him around or find another route. They were both young, but the change within the last week had shattered her expectation of him. On the other hand, it was unlikely that they'd ever be in this position again. Freya looked at Harry for the answer, then looked across at Bradley again before realising that she was going to have to make the decision by herself.

Chapter 19

The Porsche On The Driveway

The walls were closing in on Bradley. To call it a roller-coaster would be a misinterpretation as he'd simply gone from overwhelmingly rich to beyond poor in a matter of days. He'd taken out so much credit that the interest alone was going to bite him hard, and he was concerned that he'd never get it paid back in time. Freya had told him that she wasn't planning to give it back straight away and he couldn't force her, although he did think about how to get a lawyer on the way home. Pulling his phone out of his pocket, he instead turned to someone he never thought he'd need again.

"Dad?"

Explaining the situation, Bradley put his head down and spoke as though his enemies were listening in. His father sounded confused, though he was sympathetic.

"I've got to say, I would have kept the money from you, too, son. How long would it have been before you spent the lot?"

Bradley sighed. "I was only about a hundred grand in. You can buy a lot with the remaining half a million."

"A lot for other people, you mean. Were they your pals when you were skint?"

It was a cliché, one he'd heard so many times but, at that point, he was living it. Tony had once nicked a fiver he'd put on the bar waiting for a drink, all because Bradley's phone rang and he looked into his pocket to answer it. There was no proof, of course, yet his expression after he looked back spoke volumes. The silence as he thought about the incident served as Bradley's answer and his dad spoke once more.

"If you need a place to stay, you can always come back here. Don't hate Freya for what she's done, work with her and who knows, maybe you'll get it back later on tonight."

His father didn't sound convinced, yet the offer of a room was a pleasing safety net. Bradley nodded, before realising that his dad couldn't see him.

"Thanks, mate. I owe you one," he said finally.

The two of them said goodbye and hung up, after which Bradley put his phone in his pocket and drove to a roadside grill nearby to spend two pound coins that were still in his wallet from before the win. He noticed the cheapest item on the menu was a hot dog with onions priced at £2.50, and so he pleaded with the owner to accept what he had. They agreed and, within five silent minutes, Bradley had a freshly cooked meal. He loaded it with condiments, including mustard and ketchup, figuring the extras would at least help to keep him alive for a couple of hours.

Making his way back to the car, Bradley held on to his hot dog with both hands, paranoid he would drop it on the floor. He opened his door gingerly and sat in the driver's seat, looking longingly at such a simple snack. He closed his eyes and slowly started to bite into it, savouring the taste as it circled his mouth. Images of the casino filled his mind and he tried to work out where all the money had gone as he hadn't seemed to be able to keep a track on it. The whole day had been a blur and it was less clear as time went on. He felt the last mouthful of hot dog on his tongue and opened his eyes, willing it to still be there. Instead, he looked down and saw ketchup dripping down the interior of his new Porsche. Sighing deeply, he started the car and drove home.

For the first time since he'd bought it, Bradley parked his car on the driveway. It looked out of place next to their weathered, dark pink house that he'd asked his landlord to paint. He stared at the silver beast glistening in front of him, feeling some hope that he may still get to save it. He was trying to keep the thought of his debts at bay, knowing they'd be paid in an instant so long as he could make Freya realise that any money he'd won was his alone.

He was starting to feel hungry again, the days of eating plentifully causing his stomach to believe that it was a new way of life and that they'd be filling up together from that point on. Bradley looked around the house for some food, realising that there was only enough to make a couple of small meals for the two of them. Initially, he thought Freya must have binged on everything they had before realising that their shopping day was Monday and the two of them had been otherwise engaged, clearly putting themselves out of routine. It then occurred to him that Freya had been eating very little, especially since he'd started spending so much time out of the house. A pang of guilt came over Bradley and he gave up on his search, knowing he had no resources to stock up. Turning on the TV, he hoped whatever was on would distract him until Freya made it home that night.

Hour after hour passed, yet he clung on to the vision of his wife entering the house so that he could get back on track. He imagined her returning early, gradually progressing her expected time as she missed every deadline. Clearly, Harry had made her work the whole day, perhaps thinking she'd earn extra interest for herself as she did so. Harry had shown no interest in Bradley's story despite the fact it was his money though, in truth, he was simply keen to pay his debts off and see what was left.

When Freya did return an hour after her normal finishing time, she had plenty of empty food packages in tow. Bradley could see that she'd been to the same burger establishment he had when he'd first gone out and had a day of shopping, salivating at the memory of their products. Freya was unforgiving as she passed him, refusing to speak other than to advise Bradley that Harry was just a phone call away and was expecting her to let him know when they were done. Bradley had fleetingly thought they could go back to normal after working out where the money had gone before realising that it probably wasn't possible given his behaviour and tone at the showroom.

Finally, after binning her food containers and putting down her handbag, Freya sat in front of him on the chair.

"Let's talk."

Chapter 20

Bad Blood

Staring across the room, Freya and Bradley looked more like warring cowboys at their final duel than a married couple who had spent four years together. The past few days were starting to make sense for Freya, the fact Bradley had been out so much and buying clothing without mentioning money even once. Yet, she never imagined there would be a convertible sports car on their driveway. Finally, knowing she would need to be the first to speak, Freya filled Bradley in on how she'd spent her day.

"I left work at dinnertime. I had some small jobs to do, and I couldn't leave Harry piled up with cars," she said, looking purposefully into his eyes. "After that, I went to speak to a lawyer. It turns out I was wrong."

Raising an eyebrow, Bradley waited for the pause and said, "Wrong about what?"

Knowing how good her situation was, Freya spoke slowly to make sure her husband had no chance of misinterpreting her.

"I was wrong about it being your money. It isn't. It belongs to *both* of us."

The revelation hung in the air, and it visibly shook Bradley. He shook his head slowly, never looking away as he seemingly waited for the punchline.

Freya nodded her head in time with his.

"Your lack of employment meant that you've effectively used my wages from our joint account to gain your winnings. I let you use it for beer occasionally, fair enough if you lost it gambling or won a few pounds, but to win that amount and keep it from me..."

At that point, her nodding turned to shaking, again at the same rate. Freya was meticulous in her delivery, so certain about her facts that she painted an extraordinary picture.

"I was going to let you know," Bradley said, pleading with his eyes.

It seemed legitimate to him, yet his inability to tell her for almost a week was among topics of conversation between her and her lawyer.

"When would have been the best time? If I'd told you straight away, you'd never have let me go to the casino."

Freya pulled her head back inquisitively.

"You told me that was Tony's idea and yet now you're saying you wanted to go? Do you see my problem?"

She could see the cogs turning in Bradley's mind as he tried to say the right thing, so she interrupted him before he had the chance to speak.

"Just tell me what's going on. Be honest as I'm pretty sure I know most of it already."

Bradley took a breath and looked straight at Freya. "I've taken out a load of credit, some of it has interest and so I need to get it paid back. A lot of things were Tony's idea but, if I'm honest, I didn't hate them. The casino was great fun until we blew..." he hesitated, then blurted it out, "a hundred grand or so."

The sum hit Freya hard, and she visibly recoiled as though he'd attacked her with it.

"A hundred grand?!"

"Or so," he weakly reminded her. "I need to get it paid back. I'm in big trouble if I don't."

"I'm afraid it's not going to happen. I've had a hell of a week here and spent most of it wondering what you've been thinking. Now it's time for me to think of myself. The fact that you could win that amount, blow it all on a guy you complain about and try to keep me from it shows that a lot of things aren't right between us. I'm keeping the money in my account for safety. I know what will happen if I don't. You've proven that already."

Freya could see that Bradley was getting irate and reminded him that Harry was just a call away. She slowly walked away from him and climbed the stairs, making her way into their room and packing a small bag while Bradley stayed downstairs and silently sat looking at the ceiling.

Ten minutes later, Freya was ready to go. She called Harry and asked him to pick her up, giving Bradley the impression that she was staying at his house. He had nothing to say as she left, ignoring her husband and climbing into Harry's brand new yet modest saloon. They made their way to her mother's house where she was greeted with a hug, the first she'd had that week, which brought a tear to her eye. Harry watched as the tension of the situation left her body briefly, clearly helping to make her feel safe.

"I'll leave you here, yeah?" Harry asked, not moving until he got an answer.

"Thank you, love," Freya's mum said looking up, finding herself unable to take her eyes off him as he walked away.

She hugged her daughter tighter and suggested she should move in with Harry immediately. "Don't let a stud like that get away."

Freya chuckled, hoping it was a joke, but ultimately sure that it wasn't.

"I still love Bradley, I couldn't do that to him," she said quietly.

Her mum shook her head.

"After all he's done to you?"

She let go of Freya and placed her hands on her shoulders, looking into her eyes.

"I'd jump into bed with that one and send your husband a video."

"I don't think that would look very good in court," Freya suggested.

She'd fantasised about Harry on the odd occasion, shaking it off when she thought about Bradley.

"Besides, I'm still married for now. Who knows what might happen?"

Freya's mum rolled her eyes and sighed.

"If you get back with that husband of yours, you need your head checking."

Freya could only agree, although she hadn't ever imagined splitting with Bradley. Her apprenticeship had been tough, every day bringing scraped knuckles and unexplained bruises as she worked out the intricate differences between makes and models. The comfort of having someone reliable at home had kept her going, even if he wasn't a particularly hard worker. Contemplating a life alone seemed even harder, although she knew there would be money to fall back on. Whether it was enough to set her up for life was an issue for another day.

"I need a bath, then I need to sleep for a hundred years."

Chapter 21
Debt Returns

As much as Freya wanted to avoid the loneliness, Bradley felt it a hundred times more. He couldn't shake the feeling that it was his guilt, yet he knew how much Freya centred him and he needed someone to tell him when his bad ideas were really bad. Tony had been the opposite influence in his life, and he cursed himself for falling into the trap of believing some guy in a pub could be a suitable substitute for a friend.

Leaving the empty house, Bradley decided to forget everything he'd had and lost by going for a walk. He ventured through his old neighbourhood, remembering the good times when he was younger. His friends had vowed they'd be best friends forever before disappearing one by one to go to other schools, colleges, and, finally, universities. Bradley didn't want to continue in education and had eventually gone on to too many jobs he'd detested. With a black hole of debt in front of him and little chance of gainful employment, he wondered what life had in store for him. He knew he'd have to get the interest frozen on the debts or he'd never be able to pay them back, something Freya normally sorted for him. He chuckled at the thought, pushing back tears of his own making.

The car hadn't gone, a thought that entered his mind as he rounded the final corner of his childhood stomping ground. There was something he still had to do, a debt he could actually afford to pay, and so he made his way slowly back to the house.

There was nothing else to do that evening. An abyss lay in front of him, and so he grabbed his keys and jumped into his still gleaming Porsche. A cramp hit his stomach as he finally realised he'd have to give the car back to recoup some of his debts, although he promised himself he'd enjoy the drive in the meantime. Leaving the house with tyres screeching, he felt the power beneath him and yearned for as long as possible with his shiny possession as he drove back to the outskirts of town.

The grill cook was turned away from the road as he browned a fresh batch of sausages, his head only turning away from the grill when he heard the engine of the sports car pulling up outside.

As Bradley stepped out, the cook recognised him as the guy who hadn't had enough for a hot dog and turned to see if he had an order to give, subtly mentioning the Porsche. He raised an eyebrow quizzically as Bradley put his hand in his pocket and pulled out a note, twenty pounds that had been paid into his account from the benefits department, more than enough to cover his 50 pence debt. He explained his situation further, hoping to incite some sympathy and perhaps a moment of friendship from the vendor. It was easily won as Bradley omitted the finer details, particularly the fact he'd hidden it from his wife.

"Let me cook you up something," the grill cook offered softly.

Bradley shook his head, feeling the guilt surge within him again. "Thank you, but I couldn't," he replied frankly, walking away from the trailer towards his special ride.

Watching sorrowfully, the grill cook imagined winning that amount of money and thought about what he'd spend it on before returning to his sizzling stock. Over £600,000 placed instantly into your bank account. It didn't seem like the horror show his customer had just described.

A dust cloud blew up from beneath the car as it sped away once more, carrying Bradley to his final stop-off for the night. He drove for thirty minutes and arrived at the coast where he and Tony had spent the day bombing around in jet skis. He parked the car overlooking the sea, made his way solemnly to the bonnet, and sat carefully on the front of his car, watching the tide approach the beach. The waves were gentle but present, jumping as they hit the rocks at the bottom of the cliffs. He felt a blanket of calm settle over him as he took in the view, a free activity that genuinely improved his mental health in an instant. Thoughts of Freya took over and he went for his phone, contemplating sending a message to her. What to include eluded him, however.

He was interrupted by a young child, he figured late primary age, who was mesmerised by his beautiful car.

"Wow!" the child almost whispered, the shiny paintwork reflecting his curious face. "Is this yours?"

The boy's father approached behind him and chuckled, leaving Bradley to answer the question.

"Yes, it is. For now," he said, honesty finally at the forefront of his mind.

"How do I get one of these?" the boy asked in amazement, his face a picture of awe and disbelief.

The boy's father chose that moment to join the conversation.

"Hard work and diligence, son."

Bradley went bright red at the suggestion, picking up an accusatory tone in the man's voice that wasn't there. He nodded to the child, putting on his best awkward smile.

"He's right. Work hard and you'll get what you want."

The two of them carried on their journey and left Bradley to contemplate his message. In the end, he simply typed 'thinking of you x' and awaited a reply.

To his surprise, he received one—'You too.'

His heart leapt as the message came through and he smiled, genuinely this time, thinking that there was still a chance for the two of them. He'd have to work hard to regain any form of financial status, but knew he could do it with Freya by his side.

The sea whooshed in the background and was only stifled

when Bradley closed the door of the car and started the engine. He backed out of his spot and roared back to the road, turning towards his house as the darkness took over around him. A picture emerged of a beautiful house in the country, the love of his life by his side and a small, playful puppy keeping the two of them entertained.

Chapter 22

Resolution

Stepping into the courtroom, Bradley looked around at the display of statues that had been delicately carved over the years. It wasn't the ending he had hoped for, beginning with a letter from Freya's solicitors and ending with him in a thirty pound suit he'd bought with vouchers from a supermarket. There was little he'd managed to keep away from the debt collectors and bailiffs, leaving him with an almost empty flat, massive bills and nobody to share it with.

Walking in through the doors, he saw Freya in a new light. She was cold towards him, looking away as often as possible and only catching sight of him when he wasn't looking. He'd looked across hopefully after catching her in his peripheral vision, only for his heart to shatter all over again when she looked away. He'd never seen her dressed so smartly, an elegant suit with trousers and a white shirt contouring her outline perfectly. Her mother had accompanied her wearing a white, flashy blouse adorned with gold brooches, making Bradley curious about whether his remaining money was funding her lifestyle.

The judge entered the courtroom to the usual call and everyone stood as she took her seat. Bradley looked up hopefully, his puppy dog eyes grabbing her attention as she scanned the courtroom. Her expression remained unchanged as she completed her informal review and began the divorce proceedings.

Bradley had been appointed a court solicitor who had warned him that he may not be at the bottom of the barrel yet. In court, the solicitor boldly stood up and told his story, putting emphasis on the fact that he was now completely broke and living with the bare minimum. Freya's expression didn't change throughout, thoughts of her days getting oil in her eyes and tools snapping in front of her face dominating her focus. When he had finished, Bradley's solicitor sat down and made no gesture to his client, leaving him wondering if the pleas had worked.

It was then the turn of Freya's solicitor, who stood up like a freed Doberman and spoke harshly about what Bradley had put her client through. The most critical detail was the source of the money, particularly as Bradley had not been working at the time and so it was essentially Freya's wages that he had spent on BigBet. His mouth almost hit the floor when it was revealed that he owed Freya all his winnings, not just the £300,000 that he'd already spent and owed in interest. Her solicitor also told him he was lucky Freya wasn't looking to sue him for extra money due to the stress she'd endured both immediately after his win and ever since. The judge took in all of the information and nodded along, her stony expression leaving him in little doubt as to who's side she was on.

At that moment, Freya caught sight of Bradley and her façade dropped. He looked absolutely broken, the world seemingly dropping out from beneath him. Her lip quivered as she contemplated his life moving forward, especially given the luxury that she had enjoyed since their split. Although she'd not touched any of the money on advice from her solicitors, she had moved back in with her mother, enjoying the freedom of the annexe on the house, but also the dependence of having food bought for her. The money was going to make things easier upon release and she looked forward to that while the ability to leave her tough job had given her a new lease of life. Finally, she stood up and interrupted her solicitor.

"I don't want him to suffer, not like this. Don't take his money from him. It was just a selfish mistake. Let him get back on his feet with a fifty-fifty split at least."

The judge looked at Freya and asked if that was what she really wanted. Her solicitor looked incensed, both at her change of heart and willingness to suggest it in court, yet Freya was undeterred.

The details were then discussed between the two solicitors, with Bradley agreeing that Freya could keep her half of the money while he would be saved from bankruptcy. When all parties were in agreement, the judge made a closing statement.

"I think you've seen the error of your greed in this instance, although the sincerity and good nature of your wife—soon to be ex-wife—has ensured that you can pick up your life at a much faster pace. I trust you will leave this courtroom with humility and grace, particularly for your former spouse, and will grow from this experience."

The judge then brought her gavel down and dismissed the room, allowing the two parties to leave separately.

Outside the courtroom, Freya saw Bradley sat on the court steps sending a message on his phone and took a moment to speak to him.

"Everything okay?"

Freya's mother overlooked the conversation, putting her nose in the air and walking on, leaving her daughter to find her later.

"Not really. I thought this might have had a happier ending."

The words landed hard as Freya drew a breath.

"You know this was about trust, not money, right?"

A few seconds passed before Bradley nodded repeatedly, his head on a soft spring.

"So, there's no hope for us?"

"After our divorce?" Freya spoke with every ounce of surprise in her voice. "Probably not. Don't look at this as an ending, though. This is your chance to make something of yourself, whatever you want that to be."

"The beginning of a new chapter," he replied with sorrow in his voice.

He knew it would be tough to start again, particularly since he'd held a seemingly endless supply of money in his bank account, yet his options were limited. He'd also considered himself so lucky to have found and married Freya that he struggled to see how he could improve in his next relationship.

All of this was evidently none of Freya's concern.

"Take care of yourself, yeah?" she said as she walked away, still looking at him until she was forced to turn her head.

There were people everywhere outside the courtroom, all walking from left to right or right to left in front of him. Everyone was walking like they were on a mission, their pace matching their drive in their quests to secure the latest deal, even if that meant just getting coffee for the people at the meeting. Bradley perused their faces, wondering which he'd like to be next. However, the day was his and there was an entire afternoon he could dedicate to his freedom. He thought about taking life one day at a time—such a simple concept, yet so hard to achieve—and stood to walk away from the end of his wealthy life, his financial balance returned to zero.

Acknowledgments

Thanks to my wife and children, who put up with me checking sports results on family holidays. It may have felt like I was working but we got there in the end.

Also thanks to Alan Trerise and Lee Strike who introduced me to a system that kept me well away from gambling. This book was inspired while using that system.

In the spirit of the content, thanks to Indie Earth Publishing for taking a chance on my work and to Flor Ana Mireles and Damien Hanson for their editing skills.

About the Author

Terry Lander is a British author, best known for his novels *Banned*, *Alf & Mabel*, and *Red Light London*. He started writing in 2005 and has explored a number of different genres, often focusing on the unpredictability of human nature and the emotive side of his characters.

In 2017, Terry started writing children's books, starting with *Natalie's Fiendish New Headteacher*, which spawned two sequels as part of the *Natalie Underwood* series. He also co-wrote *Lewis and Bruno Face the Artificial Intelligents* with fellow author Jamie Arron.

Connect with Terry on Instagram:

@terrylanderauthor

Terry Landers

Connect with Terry on Instagram:

About the Publisher

INDIE EARTH
PUBLISHING

Indie Earth Publishing is an independent, author-first co-publishing company based in Miami, FL, dedicated to giving authors and writers the creative freedom they deserve. Indie Earth combines the freedom of self-publishing with the support and backing of traditional publishing for poetry, fiction, and short story collections by providing a plethora of services meant to aid them in the book publishing experience.

With Indie Earth Publishing, you are more than just another author, you are part of the Indie Earth creative family, making a difference one book at a time.

www.indieearthbooks.com

For inquiries, please email:
indieearthpublishinghouse@gmail.com

Instagram: @indieearthbooks

CPSIA information can be obtained
at www.ICGtesting.com
Printed in the USA
BVHW032033140423
662388BV00003B/74

9 798986 210667